A New Day
at Tanglewood

**Center Point
Large Print**

**This Large Print Book carries the
Seal of Approval of N.A.V.H.**

A New Day at Tanglewood

ANNETTE SMITH

CENTER POINT PUBLISHING
THORNDIKE, MAINE

To Jeanna

This Center Point Large Print edition
is published in the year 2007 by arrangement with
Moody Publishers.

The text of this Large Print edition is unabridged. In other aspects, this book may vary from the original edition. Printed in Thailand. Set in 16-point Times New Roman type.

ISBN: 1-58547-881-4
ISBN 13: 978-1-58547-881-1

Library of Congress Cataloging-in-Publication Data

Smith, Annette Gail, 1959-
  A new day at Tanglewood / Annette Smith.--Center Point large print ed.
    p. cm.
  ISBN-13: 978-1-58547-881-1 (lib. bdg. : alk. paper)
   1. Foster home care--Fiction. 2. Problem youth--Fiction. 3. Widows--Fiction.
  4. Girls--Fiction. 5. Large type books. I. Title.

PS3619.M55N49 2007
813'.6--dc22

2006020582

Acknowledgments

Many thanks to the following folks:

Randy, my husband, my supporter, my friend of twenty-five years.

Russell and Rachel, adult children whose humor, compassion, and intelligence make them two of the people I most love to spend time with.

My parents, Louie and Marolyn Woodall, whose other-centered lives inspire me every day.

Cheerleader friends Sheila Cook, Laura and Michael Walker, Susan Duke, Sheri Harrison, and Jeanna Lambert.

Chip MacGregor, my agent and friend.

The good folks at Moody, for putting Ruby Prairie on the map.

To God be the glory!

Chapter One

Charlotte Carter slipped into a back pew. She hated being late, though as far as she could tell, her chronic tardiness at Lighted Way Church was overlooked by most of its faithful members. These indulgent folks—and Charlotte was truly grateful for this—let her lateness, her preference for sandals and sundresses over high heels and hose, and her made-from-a-mix potluck contributions slide.

After all, Charlotte possessed what Ruby Prairie residents seemed to accept as the one perfect excuse: the sad misfortune of having been born and raised somewhere outside the Lone Star State. It had taken her until her fortieth year to make her way from her birthplace in Oklahoma to this small Texas town. In her six months at Lighted Way she'd found that even the most conservative members allowed abundant grace to "outsiders."

Tonight was the regularly scheduled second-Tuesday-of-the-month business meeting of the church. From all accounts, the January meeting was especially important for members to attend.

"Sorry," Charlotte whispered to her seatmate, Ruby Prairie's mayor and her good friend, Kerilynn Bell. She'd stepped on Kerilynn's toes trying to get to her spot. "What've I missed?"

"Not a thing. Just getting started," Kerilynn whispered back. "Everything okay?"

"Fine," fibbed Charlotte. She took a deep breath.

Estrogen-fueled crises were the norm at her house. Today had been an especially normal day.

Pastor Jock Masters, as was his custom at every Lighted Way gathering, began the meeting by approaching the Father with a moment of silent prayer.

Charlotte took advantage of the few quiet seconds to bring to God's attention the names of those sheltered by Tanglewood, the rambling pink-and-white Victorian that housed her home for troubled girls. She closed her eyes. The faces and needs of each member of her out-of-the ordinary household rolled past like credits on a movie screen.

First she mouthed the name Treasure Evans. Ample in body and heart, and full of rich wisdom, Treasure lived up to her name. Charlotte wouldn't be able to do what she did without the other woman's help. Treasure had been the friend of Charlotte's late grandmother, a friend lost for a while but now found. She had left a thriving massage therapy practice and moved to tiny Ruby Prairie to help Charlotte out with the Tanglewood girls.

When Charlotte had first bought Tanglewood, become licensed by the state, and begun taking in girls, she was determined to take care of everything without assistance from anyone in the church or in the town. Then one crisis after another hit. Without the loving help of Treasure and the folks of Ruby Prairie, Tanglewood would not have survived until Christmas. Now half a dozen girls were under Charlotte's care.

"Bless them," Charlotte prayed. "Please bless each one."

The eleven-year-old twins, Nikki and Vikki, had a mother dying of cancer and an incarcerated daddy. Their grandmother was doing all she could to care for their mother. She couldn't manage the girls, too.

Sharita, who was thirteen, was sent to Tanglewood by her parents, who lived in a gang-infested area of Houston. Sharita's older brother had been killed in a drive-by shooting, and her parents were determined to keep her safe—even if it meant sending her elsewhere to live.

Maggie, fourteen, had been found living with her mother in a broken-down van at a state park. Social Services placed her with Charlotte until her mom could get back on her feet.

Donna's mother had left when she was a baby. She and her dad had gotten along okay until he impulsively decided to take an off-shore oil drilling job, lured by the promise of quick and easy cash. The only problem was that the job would take him from home for months at a time, and Donna was left with no one to look after her. Despite her assertions that at fourteen she could take care of herself, she, too, was now a resident at Tanglewood.

Beth, fifteen, was the most troubled of the girls. In foster care all of her life, she ran away soon after her arrival at Charlotte's home. After two weeks she was found and returned, recovering from a broken foot. Though her body had healed over the past six weeks, it was the girl's spirit Charlotte fretted about. Beth was too quiet. Kept everything inside. Charlotte prayed for God to give her insight and patience in dealing with Beth.

Pastor Jock ended everyone's silent prayers with praises and requests, followed by "In Jesus' name. Amen."

Charlotte echoed his amen. When she raised her bowed head, her shoulders relaxed a bit. She let herself sink back into the pew.

Kerilynn reached over and patted Charlotte's knee, shot her a grin, and slipped her a peppermint from her purse.

Charlotte started to drop the candy into her pocket. She'd eat it later. But then again, had she remembered to brush her teeth before leaving the house? Better safe than sorry. Painstakingly, she tried to open the cellophane wrapper without making a racket. An impossible task.

"Sorry," she mouthed to Lester and Ginger Collins, sitting on her other side. She gave up on the candy. Just in case, she'd avoid breathing on anybody until she got home.

Ginger flashed her a sweet smile. Lester, who kept his pockets always well-stocked, offered her a stick of easy-to-open Juicy Fruit.

Charlotte had never belonged to a church served by a pastor as young as Jock Masters. At thirty-nine, he was a year younger than she. Nor had she known many pastors who were divorced. But she had found Jock and nearly all the Lighted Way Church members to be warm and welcoming. Catfish Martin, mayor Kerilynn's twin brother, had been cold at first. But he, too, had come around and had even been instrumental in helping Charlotte get Beth back when she ran away.

The church had embraced Treasure, too, when she moved in with Charlotte. She and Sharita were two of only a scattered handful of African-Americans in Ruby Prairie, but no one treated them ill. Lighted Way was not a perfect place, but it was full of love, and Pastor Jock preached the Word in a way that even her girls could understand.

He stood in front of his congregation now, ready to begin. Charlotte thought folks called to a meeting by the IRS would look more enthused.

First on the agenda was the quarterly budget report. Pastor Jock handed that off to Chilly Reed, church deacon in charge of finances. Chilly coughed, cleared his throat, and took hold of the report as if it were a coiled-up snake.

Chilly tried his best to speedily steer the congregation through the budgetary maze so that he could sit down. Except for a few minor bumps and detours—an unexpectedly high light bill, an increase in first-class postage—he managed to do pretty well, probably because he read so fast that lots of what he said could not be understood.

But at the mention of a rocking chair and some new wallpaper for the ladies' bathroom, folk's ears perked up.

"Whoa. Back up there, Chilly," said Catfish. "Times are tight. What are we thinking, going and spending the Lord's money on something like that? No money trees growing in the churchyard last time I looked. If we've got extra for such nonsense as that, we ought to put those funds in the bank where they can gain some interest."

"Have you seen the wallpaper we've got?" asked Nomie Jenkins.

Catfish had not.

"It's peeling. Been there twenty years at least. Half of it has come down of its own," said Ginger.

"You ever tried to nurse a baby standing up?" challenged Kerilynn.

Catfish blushed from his collar to his hairline. "Kerilynn. Please. Not in mixed company."

"Well, have you?"

Nomie cut in. "Attractive restrooms are important. It's embarrassing to direct visitors to a room that's shabby. And we should consider the needs of our young mothers. It's hard enough for 'em to get themselves and their babies to services. A rocking chair would make it much easier."

Charlotte's head turned from side to side as opposite opinions were expressed, with the split right down the gender middle. In the end, the ladies of Lighted Way prevailed, winning budgetary approval not only for a rocking chair and new wallpaper, but for a coordinating border to match.

"Any chance we could add in some new flooring?" asked Nomie, after Pastor Jock indicated it was time to move on.

"Not this quarter," answered Chilly. "'Less you ladies want to cut back on what we send ever' month to the orphans."

Which of course put an end to all that.

Chilly sat down.

Once the budget had been approved, Pastor Jock offered the floor to anyone who had a concern.

Lavada Castle raised an age-spotted hand. "We've got a problem with some of the young people in this church."

Charlotte swallowed. She imagined heads longing to turn and look at her. What were the chances the problem had to do with one of her six?

"I love every one of these children. You know that. That's why I lay it on the parents. In my day, mothers and fathers didn't allow their boys and girls to engage in such disrespectful behavior in God's house."

Charlotte racked her brain. Had some of her girls been seen passing notes? Talking during prayer?

"Somebody needs to put a stop to it," continued Miss Lavada. She looked about ready to cry.

Pastor Jock scratched his head. "I'm sorry, Miss Lavada. The young people of Lighted Way are of concern to all of us here, but I'm not sure we understand. Exactly what behaviors are you referring to?"

"Why, gum chewing, of course. Bad enough these children have gum during services, but they've been going and sticking it up under the pews. Take a look for yourself."

Like synchronized swimmers, every head in the room ducked down to inspect.

Miss Lavada was right.

Those kids.

"It's an awful mess," said Miss Lavada. "Unsanitary too."

Lester Collins stood up. "I reckon I'm part to blame. Ran into a special over at Sam's Club last time Ginger and I made a trip to Fort Worth to see the grandkids. Stocked up. Got mostly Big Red, but some Double Bubble and Juicy Fruit too. Been giving all the kids gum."

Miss Lavada sniffed.

"Didn't think nothing about it. From now on, I'll make 'em wait till after church to get their chewing gum."

"I'd appreciate that very much," said Miss Lavada.

Pastor Jock moved on. "Special event is coming up. Three and a half weeks from now we've got Friendship Sunday. It's time to be making our plans."

Kerilynn leaned over to whisper to Charlotte. "It's a day when members are supposed to bring their unchurched friends. We always have it the first Sunday in February."

"Attendance was down last year," said Nomie.

"Yes, it was," said Pastor Jock.

"I remember when we used to fill up this building on Friendship Sunday," said Gabe Eden. "In ninety-nine, best I recall, we broke 120. Had to put chairs in the aisles."

"No reason that can't happen this year," said Pastor Jock. "Though let's keep in mind that numbers aren't what we're most concerned with. Our goal is to reach out to folks with hungry souls."

"I say we do something different from our usual potluck," said Nomie. "Folks may have hungry souls,

14

but filling up their stomachs with something extra good couldn't hurt."

"We could do chili," said Alice Buck. She nudged her husband in the ribs. "Boots could cook."

"Be too cold to have it outside," said Catfish.

"Fellowship hall'd be big enough if we set up kids' tables in the classrooms," said Alice.

"I could do my fried peach pies," said Lester.

"Those pies'll bring 'em in by the droves," agreed Chilly.

Charlotte's mouth watered. She'd never tasted anything as delicious as Lester's famous fried pies, made from peaches he harvested from trees he planted and tended—all over town. Shortly after moving to Ruby Prairie, she'd looked out her kitchen window and been startled to see Lester, whom she'd barely met once, setting out four seedlings in her backyard.

"Shall we form a committee to see to Friendship Day food?" asked Pastor Jock.

"I'll head it up if y'all want me to," said Kerilynn, the obvious choice. She owned the 'Round the Clock cafe and could take care of any kitchen equipment need that came up.

Pastor Jock wrote that down. "We need someone to take charge of advertising. Do up some posters, get a write-up in the paper. We might think about getting invitations printed up for members to mail out to their friends."

"We got money in the budget for such as that?" asked Catfish. No one paid him any mind.

"I'll take that job, Pastor," said Sassy Clyde.

"Great." Pastor Jock didn't see anything else left to discuss. "That about wraps it up."

Folks started putting on their coats.

Gabe Eden raised his hand. "Can you back up a ways, Pastor? While we're on the subject of Friendship Sunday, I've got something to say. I been waiting till y'all got through to bring it up, 'cause it's big. Really big. Boots's chili and Lester's fried pies'll be a good draw, but I've got a plan that'll fill this building up. Guaranteed."

The chief of Ruby Prairie's volunteer fire department was not a man generally given to emotional displays. Tonight, though, his cheeks were red and his hands trembled. Charlotte had never seen him so worked up.

"I say we have a contest," Gabe continued. "See who can bring the most friends."

"A contest?" said Catfish. "We've never done nothing like that before."

"You mean like give out a prize?" asked Ginger.

"That's exactly what I mean," said Gabe.

"I suppose some of the rest home ladies down at New Energy could do up a granny square afghan. That'd make a good prize," said Nomie.

"A Bible commentary would be more appropriate," said Lucky Jamison.

"I reckon I could donate a heifer," said Chilly. "Motivate the youngsters to get involved. Some of them kids'll be needing 4-H projects coming up real soon."

"Y'all wait." Gabe raised his voice. "I've already got the perfect prize lined up."

16

"Gabe's got the floor," said Pastor Jock. "Let's let him speak."

"My second cousin's got a man owes him a favor. Lives down below Ella Louise. Fella's got a helicopter. Gives rides. Says he'll give us an hour of his time."

"Gabe Eden, I believe your elevator is stalled," said Catfish. "What in the world does a helicopter have to do with Friendship Sunday?"

Pastor Jock's puzzled expression said pretty much the same thing.

"We'll let whoever brings in the most friends take a ride," said Gabe. "Everybody'll want to win. Folks'll be bringing in visitors by the droves. I bet we'll have record attendance."

"Where'll it land?" asked Lester.

"I saw on TV one time where folks had to bring out their white bedsheets and make a big **X** on the ground so that one of those things would know where to set down," said Ginger. "You sure this idea is safe?"

"Won't tear up the churchyard, will it?" asked Lester. "Peach trees haven't set their buds."

"What if it's a child that wins?" asked Nomie. "I don't think many Lighted Way mothers will be inclined to let their little ones get in a helicopter with some strange man and fly off someplace they don't even know where."

"First off," said Gabe, "it's perfectly safe. It's got seat belts, and the man has a license. Has to or wouldn't be legal to fly. Second, he can land anywhere. Parking lot at the church is plenty big enough. And no. It won't tear up nothing and we won't be needing you ladies to furnish bedsheets. My guess is that it will be a child that wins the contest. Nothing wrong with that. Didn't Jesus say something about letting the little children come to Him?"

Pastor Jock confirmed that He certainly did.

"Helicopter's got room in it for three. Whoever wins gets to bring along a guest. If it's a young person, well, of course they'll bring along their mama or their daddy."

"I think it's a great idea," said Chilly.

"Baptists or Methodists never done anything like this," said Lucky.

"I think Gabe's right," said Lester. "Folks'll be trying their best to win a helicopter ride. No telling how many visitors we might have."

"Remember, our goal is to reach out to the lost," reminded Pastor Jock.

"If you preach a good enough sermon, Pastor, maybe a bunch of them'll come back and stay," quipped Keri-lynn.

"This could pump some life into this church," said Lester. "May have to think about adding on," said Nomie.

"We ain't got money for that," said Catfish.

No one paid him any mind.

"Gabe, I think everyone's in agreement. I suppose you'll let the man know we'll take him up on his offer?"

"I'll take care of all the details, Pastor," said Gabe. "We all just need to be talking this up. Let's get the kids

18

of the church excited. Friendship Sunday this year'll be one none of them forget."

Pastor Jock closed the meeting with a prayer.

Charlotte put on her coat.

"Bet you money one of your girls wins the contest," said Kerilynn.

Charlotte hadn't even thought of that.

"It'll be Maggie," predicted Kerilynn. "I've never seen a girl more outgoing. Come Friendship Sunday she'll have you picking up half the middle school in that twelve-seater van of yours. I bet you have to make two or three trips."

Charlotte turned a little green.

"You'll be the lucky one that gets to take a ride," said Kerilynn. "Have to tell the rest of us what it's like. We'll all be jealous."

And she would be sick. Terrified of heights, Charlotte had managed to avoid flying for the entire forty years of her life.

She smiled and nodded at her friend. Then silently she prayed, *Please, God, don't let a Tanglewood girl win.*

Chapter Two

Once the meeting was over and the last straggler had gone home, Jock Masters locked up the front door and went out the back. Since he lived only four blocks from the church, he'd left his truck at home, preferring a brisk night walk.

January Texas weather being as unpredictable as a church baby's cry, the residents of Ruby Prairie thought nothing of it when temperatures swung from the high seventies down into the low teens all in the same week. Tonight Jock wore a heavy jacket but needed no hat or gloves. The air was crisp and cold. Not a bit of wind blew. A full moon, white as bleached laundry, shone bright enough to make shadows of trees, buildings, and Jock himself.

He replayed tonight's gathering in his mind. Business meetings. Necessary evils. On matters of faith and grace, redemption and good works, Lighted Way folks generally agreed. It was the other, more earthly stuff that was apt to provoke a fray.

A helicopter? Oh my. Jock wasn't sure what his thoughts were on that one. Thankfully, it was the deacons who would be running the show.

Lighted Way Church wasn't a perfect place, but neither was he a perfect person. When they'd called him five years before, the search committee had liked his style of preaching but voiced suspicion regarding his status as a single man. Lighted Way had never had an unmarried pastor. Not having a wife and children gave him the freedom to devote himself to his work, they allowed, but it would make many aspects of ministry, like counseling and hospitality, more difficult.

Jock had been married once, a long time ago. It was almost twenty years since the end of the brief union, but the memories stayed tormentingly fresh. Ashley had been nineteen and pregnant. He, nineteen and foolishly surprised. When she lost the baby in her fifth month he'd felt nothing but relief. There was no more reason to be together. Right?

Ashley thought otherwise and at first had tried to get him to stay. But after enduring eighteen months of his unfaithfulness and irresponsibility, she was as ready as he to divorce.

At twenty-four, Jock became a Christian. Not until then did the magnitude of his behavior sink in. How could he have treated someone as badly as he had his young wife? What kind of person was capable of such? He felt huge regret over the lost child he'd felt no grief for at the time.

Perhaps the only child he'd ever have.

From all accounts, his ex-wife was doing fine. Remarried to a good man. Had a couple of healthy kids. But despite all that, and despite knowing with confidence he'd been forgiven for his past, Jock had trouble letting go of what he'd done. It made him leery of getting involved with women. What if there was something wrong with his character? Some ragged flaw? He dared not chance inflicting such pain on anyone ever again. Better, despite the loneliness and inconvenience of being without a mate, to stay single.

At least that's what he told himself.

Jock stayed on Main Street as he hiked toward home, past the 'Round the Clock; Catfish's combination video store, snack, and bait shop; Field of Dreams Florist; the hardware store; Angelina's Attic gift shop; Joe's Italian Restaurant; Lila's Beauty Shop; and Ruby Prairie's antique mall, Grandma Had One. The night was so quiet, and he was so absorbed in his thoughts, that he jumped when a car horn honked behind him.

"Didn't mean to startle you, Pastor. Need a ride?"

It was Charlotte Carter in her red van. Less than six months in Ruby Prairie. A widow for a year. Curly, fly-away hair and pretty blue eyes, and already an asset to the church.

"Thanks, no. Nice night to walk. Appreciate it, though. Everything okay? Figured everybody would have made it home by now."

"I ran out to the rest home for a second. Sounds silly, going out there this time of night, but I wanted to drop off some fabric scraps I've been carrying around in the back of this van for a week. Promised Miss Lavada I'd take them by for her."

"I'm sure the quilters will be pleased."

"Hope so. Sure I can't give you a lift?"

"Thanks anyway." He waved her on.

Then wished he hadn't.

When she let herself in through the back door, Charlotte found Treasure making a pan of hot chocolate.

"How was your meeting?" Treasure stirred, tasted, added more sugar.

"You ever been to a church business meeting?" Charlotte took off her jacket.

Treasure rolled her eyes. "Enough said. You want marshmallows?"

"Three." Charlotte snatched one from the bag and

22

popped it into her mouth. "Actually, it wasn't so bad. How's everybody?"

"They's fine. Maggie and Sharita are in there at the piano." She nodded to the living room. "Done run the cats off up under your bed. Peaches has been howling at them to quit, but Mavis and Jasmine seem to have taken to it. Last time I stuck my head in, them two was sitting up listening and wagging their tails like they was at some kind of a concert or something."

"The others?"

"Donna's doing her homework at the table. Not due till Monday, but she's scared she might not make an A. Nikki's watching TV, Vikki's working on that jigsaw puzzle she got for Christmas."

"And Beth?"

"Said she didn't feel good. Already went up to bed. No fever. I checked." Treasure divided the hot milk into eight mugs. "None of these girls drink enough water. Half the time they forget to take their vitamins. It's a wonder they don't all stay sick."

Cupping a mug of hot chocolate in her hands, Charlotte went upstairs to check on Beth.

Six weeks after surgery for a broken bone in her foot, some discomfort and fatigue could be expected. But Beth hadn't complained of much pain since the day of her release from the hospital. She'd learned to maneuver up the stairs with hardly any trouble at all and had gone right back to school.

Fifteen-year-old bones heal fast, the surgeon had explained. Long as she takes it easy, Beth will be fine.

"Honey, what's wrong? Is your foot hurting?"

Beth, still in her clothes, was curled on the bed on her side of the dark room. Charlotte turned on a lamp and sat down on the edge of the bed. "You need some Tylenol?"

"I'm okay." Beth shivered.

"I brought you some hot chocolate." Charlotte set the mug down. "It's only eight o'clock. Why are you already in bed?"

"I'm just tired. That's all."

Charlotte was never sure where to go from here. *Give me words, Lord. Help me out.*

The room was quiet for a long moment before Charlotte spoke. "You know what? I looked at the calendar. It's exactly two months today since the Culture Fest Parade."

Two months since Beth had run away. On the day of the parade, Kirby, a sixteen-year-old boy Beth had met at the Dallas shelter prior to coming to Tanglewood, had picked her up on his motorcycle. The two of them had hatched their runaway plan during the week they were together at the shelter.

If not for Kirby's motorcycle breaking down, Beth might have been gone for good. As things ended up, the two had stumbled upon Catfish Martin's hunting cabin less than an hour from Ruby Prairie. Townsfolk had searched all over the county looking for Beth during the time she was gone. No one would have dreamed she was at the cabin the entire time.

This much Charlotte knew. Sometime during the two

weeks she was missing, the boy had left Beth behind. On the very day that Beth was found, she'd tripped on the rickcty steps and broken her foot. Badly. Had Catfish not gone up to check on his cabin, no telling what would have happened. When she was found, Beth was in terrible pain and nearly in shock.

It took surgery and a four-day hospital stay to fix her up, but according to the doctors, she was going to be fine.

"Are you thinking about that day?" asked Charlotte. "The day you ran away?"

"I guess," said Beth.

"Other stuff too?"

"Maybe."

"You've done so well since you've been back. I'm really proud of you."

Beth looked away.

"Honey, I'm here for you. Anything you want to talk about, I'll listen."

"I know."

Charlotte took a deep breath. "Before you ran away, Beth, you seemed to be doing okay. You were settling in, doing well in school, getting along with the other girls. At least that's what I thought. I was completely surprised when you left. We all were. Honey, did something happen to make you want to leave? Was it something I did or said that upset you?"

Beth sat up in bed and hugged her knees to her chest. "No. It wasn't like that. You did everything right."

"What then? I need to know, so that if we've still got

a problem we can work through it. At first your social worker talked about another placement for you, but now Kim's decided to let you stay. I'm glad you're here, but I want *you* to be happy. Most of all, I don't want to have to be constantly worrying about you running away again."

"You don't have to worry, Charlotte. I'm not going to run. I promise."

"But you did once."

"It wasn't because of you I left. I just wanted to be—"

"With Kirby?"

Beth nodded.

"What about now?" Charlotte didn't think they were still in contact, but obviously one never knew.

"I don't know where he is." Beth chewed on a fingernail. "I don't care either."

"Because he left you at the cabin?"

"We sort of had a fight."

"You think about him a lot?"

"Not much."

"You miss him?"

"Not really." Her face didn't match her words.

"Sounds to me like you've got a broken heart. I remember how that feels. Like you're going to die. Right?"

Beth nodded.

It was time to change tacks. "You're not. I promise, because I've got a cure. Two actually. Want to hear what they are?"

"Okay."

26

"This is a prescription straight from a friend of mine, who goes by Dr. Love," Charlotte said. "First you need chocolate. Lots of chocolate."

Beth looked at Charlotte like she was crazy.

"You think I'm kidding. Here. Drink this." She handed Beth the hot mug.

Beth smiled.

"The second cure is what experts like Dr. Love call hydrotherapy."

"What's that?"

"A long bath. With bubbles. Works every time. Come on. Hop up." She leaned over and gave Beth a hug. "Let's run you a tub." Beth wiped her eyes.

"Listen, honey," said Charlotte. "You know I'm teasing with you. I understand how bad you feel. Thing is, all that's going to make you feel better is time. You can talk to me whenever you need to. You can talk to the school counselor or to Kim too. And in the meantime, you need to do things that will make you feel better. Staying up here in a dark room by yourself is not one of those things. Understand?"

"I guess so."

"Good. Now into the tub with you. Take a good long soak. Cry while you're in there, if you need to. And when you're done, come downstairs. I'll let you in on my secret, emergency stash of Hershey's miniatures for the brokenhearted. Works every time."

Charlotte stood in the hall for a moment, listening to the water run. Had she done the right thing by taking a lighter tone? There was lots going on in Beth, some things spoken, more things left unsaid. In days ahead, she hoped, more would come out. In the meantime, at least Beth was out of her room.

For tonight, that was the best she could do.

Chapter Three

Seated at Charlotte Carter's kitchen table, Treasure Evans sipped her coffee, then pushed her glasses farther up on her nose. The *Penny Saver*, Ruby Prairie's weekly shopping rag, generally proved to be a mildly entertaining and informative read. This week it contained the usual—a listing of local garage sales, Rick's Grocery Store's weekly specials, assorted livestock for sale, and several offers of lucrative employment for those interested in rewarding careers stuffing envelopes. So quickly did she scan the ads, Treasure nearly missed a new one located in the bottom corner of page four. But the border design drawn to look like a cowboy's lariat rope caught her eye. She read the ad, then read it again.

Jasper Jones's Riding School
Grand Opening January 22
Beginner, Intermediate, Advanced
Private or Group Lessons
All Ages Welcome

If that didn't beat all. A riding school in Ruby Prairie. Best Treasure could tell from the address, the place was located a couple of miles south of town.

Her mind drifted to an oft-repeated dream from her past. Dressed in a cowboy hat and western boots, she sat astride a fleet-footed chestnut mare. The horse had four white feet and a long, cream-colored mane. With Treasure snugly perched in a silver-trimmed saddle, the steed carried her over a creek, through shady woods, and across a meadow. Birds sang sweetly overhead. High in the sky, the sun shone with a gentle, filtered, warm light. Beneath the animal's feet, the grass grew tall and green while wildflowers bloomed bright as cemetery silks. The gentlest of winds blew against her back.

Her dream played like a Hallmark made-for-TV movie in which she was the ten-year-old star.

Treasure set the paper down next to her chair, then pulled off her glasses and wiped them clean on her blouse. She wasn't ten. She was sixty-two.

Still. As far back as she could remember, she'd lusted for a horse. Back then it was a dream that hadn't a chance of coming true. Raised by a daddy who drank, even as a young child Treasure had known that a person in her straits might as well set her mind on a million dollars as on a horse.

Her father was a man not given to affection, nor to the trouble of making conversation with a child. The death of her eighteen-year-old mother when Treasure was only a baby ensured that her childhood was one of aching loneliness and deprivation.

No one to talk to.

No good food to eat.

No one to insist upon daily baths, to mend rips in clothes, or to do up nappy hair.

It was the year she turned five that a bit of blessed relief came into Treasure's life. Charlotte Carter's grandma Ruby, a new bride, moved into a house just down the road and immediately showered her with kindness, even love. Though she was a white woman, in a Southern time and place when coloreds and whites didn't mix much, Miss Ruby always appeared pleased as punch to see her when Treasure, unwashed and uncared for, turned up on her doorstep for a chat. Miss Ruby would hug her, invite her inside, and give her cornbread and milk or a piece of cake.

Treasure put her elbows on the table, rested her chin on her hand. God was amazing, wasn't He? Only the Lord Himself could have orchestrated things the way they turned out. As she did many times throughout the day, Treasure said a prayer of thanksgiving to God. Who would ever believe that she would end up here, fifty-seven years later, living with Miss Ruby's grand-daughter, helping out with girls who, as she had at one time, craved a stranger's love.

It wasn't that Treasure had needed some place to stay. No ma'am. She'd done fine for herself. Divorced for nearly thirty years now, she owned her own home and had her own business, Treasure's Massage and Vitamin Therapies, back in Edmond, Oklahoma. Though the business was closed up and her house rented out, it was there in the wait whenever she decided to go back.

The timing had worked out perfectly. Doctors had warned her that if she didn't take a break from giving massages, carpal tunnel could put an end to her career. Treasure wriggled her fingers. Only lately had she felt the urge to get back to working out folk's kinks, perhaps part-time.

That was a thought. What would Charlotte think of her giving massages out of Tanglewood? There was a small, mostly unused storage room right off the kitchen, which would work really well. But then again, maybe renting space somewhere downtown would be a better idea. Maybe Lila down at the beauty shop would be interested in letting her set up in her back room.

Treasure determined to put the idea to prayer. See if God laid straight the way. But then again . . . how long did she plan on staying in Ruby Prairie? Not likely forever. Maybe the year, though that had not been her original plan.

In the meantime, wonder how old was too old for a person to learn to ride a horse? Treasure picked the newspaper back up. Wouldn't hurt to call. *Now where,* she wondered, *had those girls gone and laid the cordless phone?*

Beth checked her answers one last time before adding her paper to the growing stack of American history tests on Mr. Reynolds's desk. Had she done okay? She'd studied enough—that was for sure. Charlotte had sat with her at the dinner table for the better part of an hour three nights in a row, going over names and

31

dates and important events.

Getting so much attention was hard to get used to.

But it was nice.

Mostly.

Six weeks back at Tanglewood. It felt a little like being on a bumpy carnival ride. Some things, like having her own room and cuddling with the three Tanglewood dogs and two cats, were good. Other things, like having to go to counseling and Charlotte's watching her all the time, were not.

She wished Charlotte would quit asking her if everything was okay. She hadn't run away because of Charlotte, or because of anything about Tanglewood. All she'd thought about was Kirby and the plans they had made.

She'd never met anyone like Kirby before. On their first day together they agreed it felt as though they had known each other all their lives. At the end of the week, when he was sent to his uncle's house and she was taken to Tanglewood, Beth had thought she might die.

It was only their plan that helped her hang on.

She'd thought it would be perfect when the two of them were finally alone, with no one to tell them what to do.

Except that it wasn't.

At first Beth had loved being in the cabin with Kirby. He was really sweet and fun and protective. They'd talked about everything. But that didn't last.

At the beginning of the second week everything began to fall apart. The cabin was boring. Cold too.

They ran short on food. Kirby wanted to have everything his own way. He blamed her when anything went wrong. They began to get on each other's nerves. One afternoon they had a screaming match over who had eaten the last can of fruit cocktail. Another day Beth got so mad that she didn't speak to him or look at him for four whole hours—no small feat in a cabin less than twenty by twenty feet in size.

There was a sink that ran cold water, but no place to take a bath and no toilet. Making the trek to the woods got old really fast. Sometimes she had to go out in the dark or the rain. It was after just such a trip that, hurrying back inside the cabin, she tripped on the steps, fell, and broke her foot in two places.

It went downhill after that.

Her foot hurt.

Kirby acted like he didn't care.

They fought over what to do next.

He left.

And she was found.

Beth's foot required surgery and a four-day stay in the hospital. During that time, Charlotte stayed with her. One afternoon when they thought she was asleep, Beth overheard her caseworker, Kim Beeson, talking to Charlotte about placing her somewhere else. Maybe it would be better if Beth were placed at what Kim called a more structured facility. After all, Charlotte's loosely run home wasn't set up for kids with serious problems. It was mainly for girls who just needed a place to stay for a year or less.

It was Charlotte who had convinced Kim to let Beth stay. And Beth was so glad.

Charlotte wanted her. She wasn't going to change her mind and send her someplace else if some little something went wrong. In fact, according to Charlotte, there was nothing Beth could do to change her mind. If she was good, she could stay. If she messed up, she could stay. Charlotte grinned when she said that and told Beth she hoped she would choose to be good, but either way, Tanglewood could be her home forever if she chose.

All the same, Beth planned to be very, very good.

But being back hadn't been so easy. At first she'd been really depressed. Even though people tried to treat her nicely, she felt as though everyone was talking behind her back. Charlotte and Treasure nearly drove her crazy, asking her over and over if everything was okay. But when Charlotte said she was sorry and she'd try to give her more space, Beth wondered if she didn't care as much as she had at first.

It was so mixed up. Most of the time Beth didn't know what it was she wanted.

"Time," Charlotte had said. "It's going to take us all some time to get back to normal—whatever normal is. Before you know it, everyone will have forgotten that you were ever gone. Things will get better."

And Charlotte was right. Stuff was getting better, even though sometimes it was all still sort of weird.

And Kirby?

Beth made up her mind she didn't ever want to see him again.

"Are you worried about him?" Charlotte asked.

"No. Maybe a little. Not really."

Beth wanted to forget Kirby. But everyone else—Charlotte, Kim, and the counselor she'd gone to see every Thursday since she'd been back—kept acting as though there was something wrong with her for not wanting to talk about him.

They didn't understand. Forgetting was something a person could get really good at. A girl who has spent most of her life in foster care, one who couldn't live with her mother, a girl whose feet had never rested under the same Thanksgiving table two years in a row, got to be really good at forgetting.

Which was exactly what Beth planned to do about Kirby.

She sure hoped she got at least a B+ on her American history test.

Jasper Jones had never eaten a better piece of pie.

"More coffee?" Kerilynn stood ready to refill her only customer's cup. Two o'clock. The place was empty except for the two of them. "Please." Jasper swallowed his last bite. "Good pie."

"Crust's made with lard. You want another piece?"

"Could you fix me one up to go?" His cardiologist would not be pleased.

"Happy to," Kerilynn said. "Traveling far?"

"No. Just to my place up the road."

"Do I know you?" asked Kerilynn.

As if she really wasn't sure. Jasper smiled inwardly.

From what he'd seen so far, Ruby Prairie residents were mostly white. He sort of stood out in the crowd.

He set down his cup. "Jasper Jones. Been living here a little over a month."

"In that case, Mr. Jones, your second piece of pie is on the house." She stuck out her hand. "Kerilynn Bell. Owner here at the cafe, well as the mayor of Ruby Prairie. Welcome to town. What brings you?" She tossed her dish towel over her shoulder, pulled a chair out from an adjacent table, and sat down.

The skinny woman who made such good pies definitely wanted the scoop.

"Early retirement."

"No. You don't look old enough to retire. What kind of work did you do?"

With close-cropped hair just beginning to gray and a lean, athletic build, Jasper appeared younger than his fifty-five years. "I was a teacher. Started out in the public schools. Finished up teaching agricultural science at a little community college outside of Abilene."

"You don't say." Kerilynn scrunched her brow. "Tell me your name again?"

"Jasper Jones."

Kerilynn paused. "Now I know who you are. The riding school. Saw your ad in the *Penny Saver*. Couldn't figure out who that was."

"Grand opening's next week. Hope lots of folks come."

"They will. Ruby Prairie folks don't want to miss a thing. And they love grand openings."

"I'm hoping they'll want to sign up for lessons," said Jasper.

"You serving refreshments?" asked Kerilynn.

"Coffee and doughnuts. Sodas for the kids."

She studied her thumbnail. "You thought about doing hot dogs?"

"No."

"Hot dogs always go over big."

Chapter Four

Plans for Friendship Sunday were proceeding at a dizzying pace.

Lester and Ginger Collins made a trip to Sam's Club so as to stock up on the sugar, flour, and oil he'd be needing to make all those legendary fried peach pies. No one at Lighted Way was to know, but Lester's dessert donation was coming at great personal cost to both him and his wife. Twice a week, he cooked up a fresh batch of pies. Every morning for the past fifteen years, he and Ginger had finished off their breakfast with the sharing of a fried peach pie while listening to Paul Harvey on the radio.

Back in the summer, Ginger helped him put up a precisely figured nine bushels of his peaches, enough for their personal needs, plenty for the pies he sold every fall at Ruby Prairie's annual Culture Festival, and a fair amount for pies to carry to the sick and bereaved.

Since he'd not allowed for the extra peaches needed to make pies for Friendship Sunday, his and Ginger's personal supply would be completely depleted.

"You do know," explained Lester, "there won't be any more pies from now until the first crop of peaches is ready to pick. Probably late June, could be July."

"We've been blessed, Lester," said Ginger. "Won't hurt us to sacrifice for the good of the church."

"I just want to be sure you and I are together on this."

"Of course we are. Besides, we've both put on some pounds this winter."

Lester was silent. He thought a little bit of weight became a woman.

"Short folks like us can't be carrying extra pounds. Cutting out those pies will do us both some good."

She was right, of course.

They put it to prayer.

"Lord, help us to give these pies with open hearts."

Sassy Clyde, in charge of advertising and promotion, bought a new program for the old computer she used for keeping her records at her antique mall, Grandma Had One. On the shelf at the store, it had looked to be just the ticket she needed to produce the eye-catching flyers, posters, and invitations she had in mind. *Simple Installation,* the package read. Simple, says who? Thing was so complicated, trying to get it to work Sassy nearly lost her religion, as well as her antique inventory records. In desperation, she finally called her sixth-grade grandson, Nick, to come down and help her get it set up. Which of course he did in about ten minutes.

Then Sassy was off on a roll.

"Makes all kinds of posters, cards, and flyers," she told Pastor Jock on the phone. "Thing's got pictures of everything under the sun. Borders and, oh, all sorts of designs you can do. I'll make us up some samples. Run them down to you this afternoon. You can pick out whichever ones you like the best."

Boots Buck and Kerilynn were working in tandem, lining up the food. "How many should we plan on, Pastor?" Kerilynn called to inquire.

"The highest recorded attendance I can find was 122," he told her.

"I'm thinking we may beat that," said Kerilynn, "what with Lester's peach pies and Gabe's cousin's friend's helicopter. Don't you figure we ought to plan on 150? Whatever's left we can carry over to New Energy. Martha down there's a pretty good cook, but I know those poor souls get tired of the same old thing."

"Good plan. Anything you need me to help with?" asked Pastor Jock.

"Not a thing," said Kerilynn. "Boots and I have got it under control. Besides, you're the one what's got the biggest job. We may be making up food for the body, but you're delivering up food for the soul. By the way, what's the topic of your sermon going to be?"

"Not set yet," said Pastor Jock. "Working on a couple of ideas."

"You're not preaching about giving, are you?" asked Kerilynn. "I hadn't planned on it."

"Good," said Kerilynn. "You know how visitors hate that."

"Not like Lighted Way members, who love sermons about money," Pastor Jock teased.

"Be seeing you, Pastor." Kerilynn let his comment slide with a smile.

During her first year of married life, Rose Ann Eden kept up a running case of hurt feelings. No matter what she did to please her young husband, nothing seemed to work. She would make Gabe a wonderful meal, sit across from him, and watch as forkful after forkful went into his mouth. When she'd ask him how everything was, his reply was always the same. *Fine,* he'd say. *Just fine.*

When she would get herself all dressed up to go out, do her hair and her nails all just so, she would toss him a flirtatious smile and ask him how she looked. *Fine, honey,* Gabe would say. *You look just fine.*

He said the same thing when she cleaned the house till it sparkled, when she painted their bedroom his favorite color, and when she knitted him a scarf with her own two hands. All of it was deemed *fine.*

While all those *fines* just about broke Rose Ann's heart, they prompted her to strive even harder to please her new husband.

It was not until Gabe and Rose Ann had been married a good ten months that, after finding his wife crying curious tears three times in one week, easygoing Gabe finally explained to his wife that fine to him was, well, just *fine.* About as good as it got.

40

"But what about *wonderful, delicious, beautiful?*" Rose Ann had asked. Wasn't that the same as *fine?*

Rose Ann had come to accept that, according to even-tempered Gabe, it was. Her husband was not a man given to emotional highs or lows. He rarely got upset. He never got depressed. He limited his expressions of joy or humor to miss-if-you-blinked, twinkly-eyed smiles.

One time, over coffee, Rose Ann's neighbor had attempted to describe the temperament of her dog, a polite, old-lady Labrador retriever. She said her sweet pet was so gentle she imagined you could set her on fire and the dog still wouldn't bite. Rose Ann had set her mug down and nodded complete understanding.

Which made Gabe's unprecedented excitement over Friendship Sunday so impressive. Rose Ann had never seen him so worked up.

Seemed every morning at breakfast he thought of something else to tell the man, another detail he had forgotten to ask about. *What time you going to be here? Yes. That's good. Won't set down until after Pastor Jock has done finished his sermon. Right. Which direction will you be coming from? The east? Yes, sir. That will work. Vacant lot next to the church will be clear. No. No power lines anywhere near. They run on the other side of the church. How long will you be flying when you go back up? Will they be able to see us if we wave from the ground? You will stay and have chili with us, won't you, sir?*

Rose Ann hoped Gabe didn't worry the man to where he changed his mind about coming at all.

• • •

Pastor Jock turned off his phone. Time for some one-on-one with the Lord. He'd been pondering what exactly to preach about when Friendship Sunday came around. Lots of folks would be coming who didn't usually make it to church. His sermon needed to be positive and uplifting, but powerful and true to the Word.

Lord, guide me. Show me what You would have me say. Prepare me, Your servant, for this task.

He was sitting quietly in his chair, eyes closed, concentrating on his prayer, when someone began to pound on his closed office door.

"Pastor? You here? Wait till you see what I've fixed up on my computer!"

Charlotte slid a pan of slice-and-bake peanut butter cookies out of the oven. Did she have enough milk? What about juice? She checked the refrigerator. In ten minutes, six hungry girls would descend upon Tanglewood's kitchen.

Five months ago she'd begun serving as fill-in Mom to the girls. Possessed of a fiercely independent nature, for the first couple of months Charlotte had been determined to run Tanglewood without help from anyone else. But the citizens of Ruby Prairie insisted that they not only *know* all of her business but help her out with it as well.

Thanks to Kerilynn's organizational skills, three mornings a week a pair of ladies came to help out. With their energetic help, Tanglewood's two stories stayed reasonably clean and the girls' laundry was generally caught up. Saturdays, good-hearted men arrived to take care of Tanglewood's acre-plus yard and do any necessary maintenance on Charlotte's twelve-seater Ford van.

Now that she'd gotten accustomed to her new friends' labors of love, Charlotte couldn't imagine getting along without their help.

Treasure, too, was an enormous blessing. Charlotte thanked God every day that her friend had decided to stay on.

"You're outnumbered, sugar." Treasure had set her straight. "An extra pair of eyes and an extra set of ears is what this house needs." She'd been 100 percent right.

Though any house with so many girls was bound to be crazy much of the time, Charlotte was living out her dream of taking care of a big bunch of children. It was what she had wanted, in spite of never having children of her own, for all of her life. Only one thing was missing. Her husband, J.D., eleven months gone, would have loved all this as much as she did. How different things would have been if not for the cancer that had taken his life. For one thing, she had a feeling he wouldn't have gone along with her painting Tanglewood pink with white trim. Not only that, but if J.D. were around, the home might be full of rowdy boys instead of moody girls.

"You making cookies?" Treasure, drawn downstairs by the warm aroma, bustled into the kitchen.

"Sort of. Slice-and-bake," said Charlotte. She held out a cookie-laden spatula.

"Hard to believe store-bought can be this good," said Treasure. She broke the hot cookie and popped half into her mouth. "Course nothing's good as homemade. Speaking of which, I hear Lester Collins is doing up dessert for Friendship Sunday. He a good cook?"

"Makes the best fried peach pies in the world," said Charlotte. She sat on a kitchen stool, waiting for the next batch to get done. "I've only had them once—at the Culture Festival in November. But believe me, I haven't forgotten. They're the best."

"Folks at the church are saying his pies will draw lots of visitors in. Course the helicopter's what's really going to do it. When I carried the girls to school this morning, they talked about it all the way there. I think Sharita's invited half the middle school."

She pulled her keys from her purse. "Why don't I pick them up as well today? If that little social worker comes early, you'll be here to let her in."

Kim Beeson? Coming today? Charlotte looked at the calendar. Sure enough. "That would be great. It slipped my mind she was coming today."

Treasure left out the back door. "Don't let that next batch burn," she called over her shoulder.

Treasure put the van in park but kept the engine running and the radio playing while she waited for the girls to come out. She'd brought along the *Penny Saver* so she could take another look at the riding school ad. After reading it for about the fifteenth time, she made up her mind. Soon as she got home she would give Mr. Jasper Jones a call.

Maybe she was too plump, or maybe he would charge her too much. Maybe she was too old to ride a horse.

But maybe she wasn't.

Even if it turned out she couldn't learn to ride, surely the man would let her come out and see his horses, pet them, maybe watch other folks ride.

The school bell rang, and Treasure put the *Penny Saver* back into her purse. The double outside doors sprang open, and students began streaming toward the waiting school buses and cars.

First came Nikki and Vikki. How did Charlotte manage to always tell those two apart? If she studied them closely, Treasure could usually get it right, but if she was in a hurry or if they were trying to pull a fast one on her, she mixed them up every time.

Next was Donna. Long brown hair, slightly built. That girl was getting prettier every day. She sure did miss her daddy, though. Appeared to Treasure that he was the one who was missing out.

Sharita, prissy and loud. Full of fun. Child was trying to grow her hair out into dreadlocks. As if being one of the few African-American students in the Ruby Prairie school system didn't make her stand out enough already. She and Maggie, best friends since arriving at Tanglewood on the same day, sure made a pair.

That Maggie. Red-haired and freckle-faced. Raised up in the woods by folks who on any given day might have more old cars in the yard than teeth in their heads. From what Charlotte said, *rural* didn't even begin to describe her background. No indoor plumbing, but satellite TV was how Maggie described her grandma's house. Charlotte had done a lot toward teaching Maggie manners and how folks in Ruby Prairie were expected to keep clean. The child was doing better, but she still had a ways to go.

Today Beth was the last one to head toward the van. Treasure saw her speak to several other students as she walked past them. She smiled and walked with her head up. From the looks of it, she was at least beginning to put those two weeks with that boy behind her.

Treasure agreed with Charlotte's observations that Beth was truly giving Tanglewood and Ruby Prairie a chance. And while her running away had been a heart-wrenching, terrifying event when it was happening, from the looks of things God had taken a bad situation and brought good from it.

Just like Him to do such a thing. Treasure had seen it many a time.

The girls piled into the van.

"Where's Charlotte?" asked Nikki, then Vikki in turn.

"Howdy do to you too!" said Treasure. "She asked me to pick you girls up. Kim's coming today. She might already be at the house. How was school?"

"Hi, Treasure. Where's Charlotte?" First Beth, then Maggie, Sharita, and Donna.

"At home. Waiting on a visit from Kim."

The girls were fond of her, but they were crazy about Charlotte. She had, after all, been the one who had taken them in at the beginning. Treasure didn't take offense. Her presence was an important contribution to the running of Tanglewood. She knew it and Charlotte knew it. That was more than enough.

Charlotte opened the door for Kim. "Come on in. Girls'll be home soon. How was your drive?"

The young social worker, fresh out of school and usually a bit disheveled, never failed to spark maternal feelings in Charlotte. Little more than half her age, Kim was good, if not always sure, at her job. Today she looked harried, as though she'd already put in a full day.

"Need a pit stop?"

"Always. Thanks." Kim dropped her bulging satchel on the floor by the stairs and hurried toward the bathroom.

Charlotte noticed the hem was coming out of the back of her skirt.

It was the chaos of hungry home-from-school girls that greeted Kim in the kitchen.

"Y'all are like a herd of baby goats," Treasure chided, as the girls clamored for cookies and juice and milk.

"Kim's here," said Charlotte.

"Hi, Kim."

"Hey, girls. How's it going?"

They were accustomed to her monthly visits. Only Beth hung back a bit when the others gave her hugs.

"You want some cookies?" asked Maggie.

"I'll get you some milk," said Donna.

"Thanks, but I'm not staying long today."

The girls were settling down. All of them were by

now either sitting around the table or leaning up against the kitchen counter.

"Looks like you all are doing fine. Charlotte, if everybody's okay, I mainly just need to talk to you."

"I'm not okay." Maggie spoke through a mouthful of cookie. "I've got a rash."

"You've got nothing more than a mosquito bite," said Treasure.

"I need to talk to you about my dad," said Donna.

Kim locked eyes with Charlotte.

Treasure spoke up. "Honey, I forgot. There's a letter came for you today. Looks like it's from your daddy. I laid it on your bed upstairs."

Donna forgot all about needing to talk to Kim.

"What's up?" Charlotte and Kim sat in the living room on opposite ends of the room's ticking-striped couch.

"My usual monthly report," said Kim.

"That's all?" Charlotte didn't think so.

"That and one more little thing."

Charlotte waited.

"How's Beth?"

Charlotte relaxed. This time she had nothing but good to report. "She's doing much better. Talking to me. Going to the counselor every week. Teachers say she's speaking up in class, and her last set of grades was good. She tried out for a part in a play at school. Beth doesn't know it yet, but she got it. Her teacher was so thrilled she called me today on her conference period. She's eating well, sleeping well, and not complaining of those headaches she had when she first came."

"That's great." Kim chewed on the end of her pen.

"Truthfully, it took a while, and I had my doubts," said Charlotte, "but lately Beth doesn't even seem like the same girl."

Kim pushed a stray lock of hair behind her ear. "I'm glad to hear all that, because I have some exciting news."

Charlotte listened.

"Beth is being considered for admission into a special program for disadvantaged students. It's called Wings of Gold. An unbelievable opportunity. She'd have all the advantages of a top-notch private school as well as the opportunity to pursue any of the fine arts she shows interest in."

"But she's only been back a few weeks. When did this come up?" asked Charlotte.

"Beth was nominated way back before she ran away," said Kim. "Truthfully, I'd forgotten all about it until yesterday, when I got a letter saying she's made the first cut."

Charlotte felt slightly confused. "I didn't know there was anything like that here in Ruby Prairie. When does the program start? Would she still be in some of her same classes?"

"Charlotte, Wings of Gold is not in Ruby Prairie." Kim was so excited she could barely get the words out. "It's not even in Texas. If Beth gets in, she'll be going to Colorado Springs."

Chapter Five

Beth—leave Tanglewood? Charlotte didn't know what to say.

Kim thought it best not to tell Beth at all unless she was accepted, but Charlotte wasn't convinced. How long before they would know if she got in? A couple of days? Maybe five? That was a long time not to tell.

When Kim was ready to leave, Charlotte followed her outside. She stood coatless, shivering on the porch. Kim hugged her good-bye, then hurried down the side-walk. Charlotte didn't move from the porch. She watched as Kim opened and closed the yard's low white gate, then got into her car.

Even after the taillights of Kim's car were out of sight, Charlotte stalled. In the late afternoon's waning light, she plucked dead leaves from a potted plant, brushed fallen leaves from the seat of a wooden rocking chair, and straightened the pillows on the wicker porch swing.

Beth wasn't a small child. Didn't she have a right to know about plans being made on her behalf? Then again, what if such shocking news caused her to bolt, to run away again, or worse—to pull back into that shell she had only begun to cautiously crack?

Through the lace curtains hung on either side of Tan-glewood's front door, Charlotte could see the girls hud-dled around her kitchen table. Somebody must have spilled milk, most likely one of the twins. She could see

Treasure wiping at the table with a rag. Sharita, ever the drama queen, was standing up and entertaining the rest. The other girls and Treasure were all laughing.

Standing there, looking in, Charlotte decided Kim was right. She would not say anything to Beth. She needed time to think, to pray, to get used to the idea of Beth being gone. And who knew? She might not even be accepted to the program.

Homework. Supper. Choir practice. Just another busy evening lay ahead. Not until she had her hand on the knob of Tanglewood's front door did the surprise sob catch in Charlotte's throat. Years had not made the thought of being left any easier to bear. First her parents' deaths when she was eighteen, then J.D.'s. Every time she was faced with the leave-taking of someone she loved, overwhelming feelings of sadness and unease came over her.

It's not about me. It's about Beth. What's best for her. Charlotte swallowed hard, took some deep breaths, then wiped her eyes and dug in the pocket of her jeans for a tissue to blow her nose.

Planting a smile on her face, she walked into the house.

Treasure could not make up her mind. If a person didn't own actual cowboy boots, which was the better substitute—cute little imitation lizard leather church boots with stacked two-and-a-half-inch heels, or clunky leather low-heeled lace-ups bought in like-new condition for three dollars at Lester and Ginger Collins's fall yard sale? Hadn't she read somewhere that you were supposed to wear boots with a heel, so as to keep your feet from falling out of the stirrups? Best then to go with the church boots. Besides being the most attractive choice, they were already broken in.

Jasper Jones had sounded very nice on the phone.

"Yes, ma'am. I give lessons to folks of all ages. . . . Why, of course not. I haven't met a person yet who was too old to learn to ride. . . . No. I'm not officially open yet. Chamber of Commerce is coming next week to do my grand opening, but you come right on. All that's just formalities. . . . How about tomorrow. Say two o'clock?"

Treasure hadn't told Charlotte about the lessons. In spite of her excitement, she felt a little sheepish about wanting this thing as badly as she did. Even to her, the idea seemed crazy. Most women her age who decided to take up a new hobby settled on something like quilting or scrapbooking. Maybe water aerobics or tennis, if they were thin and more daring. Until she knew for sure how it would go, she would just as soon keep her plan to herself.

On the day of her first lesson, Treasure put on her boots and what she hoped were appropriate riding clothes.

"New pants?" Charlotte's mouth dropped open, and she looked Treasure up and down.

"Naw. I've had 'em awhile. Just don't wear them very often."

Up until the first cold snap, Treasure had worn bright

sleeveless print patio dresses every day. When the weather turned colder, she had switched to oversized jewel-toned tunic tops paired with coordinating elastic-waist slacks.

Today's attire, stretch denim jeans and a pearl snap shirt, was a bit of a departure.

"Okay. Tell me the truth." Treasure spilled the beans. "I'm going out to that man's place what's got the horses. Remember that ad in the paper? You think I look all right?"

"Lessons?"

"Yes. Horseback riding. Western style."

"You're going today?"

"Unless you tell me you need me to do something round here. I'll be back by the time the girls get home from school, or at least soon after. You're picking them up today, aren't you?"

"Why, sure. No. I don't need you. And you look cute in those jeans. But why didn't you tell me you'd signed up for horseback riding lessons?"

"Pshaw. It's not no big secret. Just seems kind of silly, an old woman like me. Thing is, ever since I was a little girl I've wanted to ride. You think I'm too old to start out?"

"Why, no! I think it's wonderful. What time is your lesson?"

"Two." Treasure looked at her watch. "Lands. I'm going to be late. Maybe I ought to call the man up and tell him I'll come next week."

"No, ma'am," said Charlotte. "You go get in that van

53

of yours and get yourself out to his place. Just don't get hurt."

Treasure did as she was told.

Lots of folks had come to Pastor Jock with ideas about what he should preach about on Friendship Sunday.

"Preach about patriotism," was Catfish Martin's strong suggestion. "America, love it or leave it. Folks today don't understand what perils this great nation of ours is up against. People don't even stand up during the national anthem like they ought. I saw grown men keep their hats on when the Boy Scouts carried the flag past them at the Culture Fest Parade. Oughta be ashamed."

Pastor Jock had it on good report from Kerilynn that Catfish stood up in his living room when the national anthem was played on TV. Though patriotism was not exactly what he had in mind, Jock was not inclined to argue with the man's dedication.

Catfish had more ideas to share. "Pastor, we could even give away miniature flags to the first fifty visitors. Personally, I'd be willing to chip in an extra twenty dollars to go toward that. Give it some thought, will you, now?"

Pastor Jock promised that he would.

"A woman's place is in the home." Lucky Jamison had made a special trip to Jock's office on her way home from visiting her sister at the New Energy Rest Home, so as to tell him what she believed the community needed the most. "These young women need to be told to keep house and take care of their husbands instead of running around trying to be policemen, firemen, all such as that. No wonder so many of these children don't know how to behave. Preach about the family, Pastor. These young mothers need to hear it."

"Abortion, homosexuality, pornography," urged Dr. Lee Ross, deacon at Lighted Way and Ruby Prairie's well-respected veterinarian. "Terrible problems. Community needs to be informed. I've got some articles I'll give you, if you need a place to start."

Pastor Jock promised to give everyone's suggestions lots of thought and prayer. In the end he decided to go with a sermon about the Prodigal Son.

"I can see where you come up with that," said Catfish. "You still want me to collect for flags?"

"That's one of my favorite stories in the Bible," Lucky Jamison approved.

"Sound topic. Be a good message for the unchurched to hear," said Dr. Ross.

Pastor Jock was relieved but not surprised at their generosity. While at most any given time, some type of church stew could be found simmering within the ranks, most Lighted Way folk were good-hearted, if opinionated, folks who truly loved the Lord. Early in Jock's ministry, he'd learned that apathy and disinterest were much harder to combat than controversy. Given a choice, he'd take a strained church over a sleeping one any day of the week.

Lacing up his running shoes, Jock allowed that there was one drawback to the goodness of Lighted Way

Church members. Not only were they possessed of generous spirits, but they'd proven themselves extremely generous with their offerings of holiday goodies. The pastor's love of sweets was known by all of Ruby Prairie's very best cooks, evidenced by the proliferation of banana puddings, chocolate pies, and old-fashioned tea cakes at every potluck.

Several times a week, beginning Thanksgiving week and extending into the first week of January, assorted goodies had been hand-delivered to his office and his house. Date nut bread and applesauce cake for breakfast, lemon bars and raspberry jam prints for lunch, peanut butter fudge and cherry pecan divinity for bedtime snacks.

"Gone a little fleshy on us these days, haven't you, Pastor?" Gabe had said last Sunday.

"Put on a few pounds over the holidays, have we?" said Nomie. Shoot. He had.

So now, in these middle days of January, Pastor Jock found himself paying the price of his indulgences, trying to dispense with his uncomfortably expanded middle. He'd managed to drop three pounds in the past seven days. Five more to go. From past experience he knew they would be the ones that clung most tightly to his gut.

His weight-loss plan included cutting back on carbs and taking five-day-a-week morning jogs. Yesterday he'd gone to the high school track; today he'd slept too late. School was in session, and the PE classes would be using the track. He opted instead to go to the cemetery, a site preferred by in-the-know Ruby Prairie exercise enthusiasts.

Like Pastor Jock, Charlotte had learned that running or walking the blacktop road that meandered through the graves of Ruby Prairie's cemetery was an acceptable thing to do. Not a sign of disrespect.

"Why, everybody walks at the cemetery," Kerilynn had told her when Charlotte had gone to her to make sure. "Long as you don't carry on or take a boom box, it's fine. Good place to think. Not too crowded. If you make the whole loop, you'll have gone three-quarters of a mile."

No matter what time of day or day of the week that she put on her running shoes, Charlotte knew she'd have the company of a handful of folks.

The cemetery was an old one. Gravestones went back to the late 1800s, when Ruby Prairie was first established. The road that twisted its way around the solitary place was set on a slant—actually, the perfect slight aerobic incline.

And Kerilynn was right. The cemetery was always the perfect place for a person who needed to think.

Or to talk.

"Good morning." Pastor Jock pulled up in his truck just as Charlotte got out of her van.

"Hi, there. Getting some exercise?"

"Little bit," he answered. He got out and began to stretch. "You?"

"My New Year's resolution. I just walk, though. Don't you run?"

She'd seen him making rounds on the track at the school.

"Usually. But I'm walking today too," he replied. "Pulled a muscle yesterday. Want some company?"

"Sure."

Pastor Jock and Charlotte Carter had not even sweated it two times around the cemetery road before they were spotted. By noon, the regulars at the 'Round the Clock got the word.

"You hear? Pastor Jock and Charlotte Carter are keeping company."

"No! Really?"

"How long?"

"Not sure."

"Couple of weeks, I heard."

"Longer than that."

"You reckon they'll get married?"

"Wouldn't be a bit surprised."

Chapter Six

Jasper Jones looked at his watch, looked up at the sky, looked up and down the road that ran in front of his place. Ten after two. Stood up by his first student? That didn't bode well. Even Belle, the oldest and most even-tempered of his six horses, was growing impatient. Not happy to be called in from the pasture to be saddled in the first place, after a few minutes tied to the corral she'd stuck her ears back and begun to paw at the ground. Now thoroughly peeved, Belle had gone to gnawing on the board fence.

"Quit that." Jasper scratched the mare's chin. "Don't you be messing with my new fence." She raised her head. That was when he heard the sound of a vehicle turning into the drive. "Look there. We were giving up too soon. Bet that's our student now."

Maybe not. The vehicle was an old delivery van, painted blue, and looked not to have any backseats. The van pulled in and parked, the door opened, and the person who had to be his new student got out.

Cute black woman. Carrying a big old red purse. Not as far up in years as she'd led him to believe. Late fifties maybe. A little on the plump side, but not too bad. Hair fixed real nice.

"Good afternoon, ma'am. Jasper Jones. See you made it all right."

"Yes. I did. Thank you." She offered her hand. "I'm Treasure Evans, and I'm so very sorry I'm late. It's my fault, and of course I'll still pay you for the full hour."

"Not a problem. Pleased to meet you." Jasper shook her damp palm and politely ignored her comment about his fee. "So you're looking to learn how to ride. Come to the right place. You ever been on a horse before?"

"Never. I'm a little nervous. You think you can teach someone like me?" She was short, and when she looked up at him, she squinted in the afternoon sun.

"No reason why not. Let's see now. Belle here is already saddled. How 'bout we put your purse right inside the barn? Got a hook we can hang it on. That be all right?" He led Treasure inside a freshly painted building that smelled of hay and leather and horse manure.

Only when she was inside the barn did Jasper get a good look at her boots.

"Did you bring any other shoes?"

"These won't work?"

"What size you wear?" He didn't want to hurt her feelings, but those were the silliest boots he'd ever seen. Such as that could get hung up in the stirrups. Be dangerous. Rubber-soled sneakers would have been better.

"Eight. Well, really eight and a half or nine," she said.

"Same as my mother used to wear. Tell you what. You wait right here. I believe I've got a pair'll fit you." Jasper strode across the grass and disappeared into the house, letting the screen door slam behind him. Once he'd gotten what he needed, a pair of like-new ladies' cowboy boots in a roomy size nine, he came right back. "These haven't hardly been worn. Want to try 'em?"

She got sort of an odd look on her face. Women could be funny. Maybe this one was opposed to putting on used shoes.

"They're clean," Jasper said.

She didn't look too sure—actually took a step back. He tried again.

"Ever go bowling? No different from wearing rented shoes at the bowling alley."

"I appreciate the offer." She held the boots out from her like they were a snake or something. "Your mama

60

". . . is she . . . I mean, how long has she been—?" Treasure stumbled over her words.

So that was it. Jasper laughed out loud. Woman thought he was offering her his dead mama's personal effects. "Don't worry. My mama is just fine. She's in Arizona. In excellent health. Left her boots with me. Don't know why I moved them all the way here, but I did. If they fit, you can have them."

Treasure laughed too, revealing a dimple.

"I didn't mean to be ungrateful. These boots are wonderful. Very generous of you to offer them to me. But what about your wife? Can't she wear them?"

"I guess she might could. Problem is I haven't found her yet." Treasure looked up from where she was sitting, putting on the free boots.

"Not married," he said.

"Divorced?"

"Nope. Never been married ever. You?"

"Once. Divorced more'n thirty years." She stood up.

"How do those feel? Should be snug but not too tight."

"Feel good."

"All right then, you ready to get started? Let me introduce you to my friend here. Her name's Belle. She's a gentle horse, but like all animals, she can be skittish with folks she doesn't know. Walk up real easy. That's it. You'll want to approach her from her left side."

Fifteen-year-old Beth, sitting in Mrs. Price's English class, chewed the pink polish off of her left thumbnail.

61

Her stomach felt funny. She laid her head on her desk and wondered if Mrs. Price would give her a restroom pass.

It was a good thing Mrs. Price had given them time to do free reading. No way would she have been able to concentrate on any written work. All day long the feeling inside had swollen until she could barely think about anything else. If this hadn't been the last period of school, Beth didn't know what she would do.

Adults didn't give kids enough credit. Treated them sometimes like they couldn't see or hear. No way could you live in a string of foster homes all your life and not get a sense for when people weren't telling you stuff. Like last night. That whole visit with Kim had been sort of weird. And after Kim had left, Charlotte sure took her time coming in. It all had something to do with her, Beth was sure of it.

Had she done something wrong?

What could it be? She'd been trying really hard. Her grades were good, and she'd not even fussed about having to see that counselor who had the bad breath and wore those same ugly shoes every single week.

What if Charlotte decided that she couldn't stay at Tanglewood anymore? What if she had to go back to the shelter? And what if Kirby was there?

She didn't even want to think about that.

Tanglewood was a really pretty house. And Charlotte was a good person. She wasn't a very good cook, but since Treasure came to help out, meals had gotten lots better. Six girls were a lot, but she'd lived in some foster homes where there were more. Ten one time. Boys too. At least there weren't any boys at Tanglewood. Sometimes the other girls got on her nerves, especially Maggie and Sharita, but the twins were really cute. She loved it that Tanglewood had dogs and cats. For the past three nights Snowball had slept in her bed. Everybody knew Snowball didn't like anybody but Charlotte.

And her.

Please, God. Don't let me have to leave.

Whatever it was she was doing wrong, she would try to do better. Beth began to chew on a new nail.

"So." Kerilynn stood next to Pastor Jock's booth with her hand on her hip. "How's Charlotte?"

"Excuse me?" Since he'd run the past five days in a row, Jock was forgoing his dietetic grapefruit and oatmeal breakfast in favor of the special at the 'Round the Clock: two eggs over easy, hash browns, and biscuits.

"Charlotte," repeated Kerilynn. "How is she?"

"Fine, I guess. Why? Is she sick?" He wished Kerilynn would go ahead and take his order.

"I suppose some folks might call it that," Kerilynn said with a wink. "In which case, you're looking a little bit peaked yourself. Might need to see a doctor."

What was this all about? Charlotte had seemed fine at the cemetery two days ago. Perhaps one of the Tanglewood girls was sick. How had he not heard?

Ignoring her cafe customers' empty coffee cups, as well as Nomie Jenkins standing at the cash register ready to pay, Kerilynn sat herself down right across from Jock. "You two getting along pretty good, sounds like. No need to be embarrassed, Pastor. Everyone thinks it's a wonderful thing. Been wondering why it was taking you so long to get together in the first place. You and Charlotte make a perfect couple."

Nomie looked over at Kerilynn, saw she wasn't coming to take her money anytime soon, counted out what she owed, laid it out by the register, and left.

Jock's mouth dropped open. "Kerilynn, I don't have a clue what you're talking about. Me? And Charlotte Carter? What gave you the idea we were a—well, a *we?*"

"Aren't you seeing each other?"

Lucky Jamison got up and fetched the coffeepot and started making rounds filling the customers' cups.

"Not unless church counts. In that case I'm seeing you, too, well as Gabe, Chilly, Catfish, Nomie, Miss Lavada, and on a good Sunday about eighty-five others. Where did you get the idea I was *seeing* Charlotte Carter?"

"Lester Collins saw you and Charlotte at the cemetery together day before yesterday. He was out there tending to his peach trees. He came in here for lunch and let it slip he saw you and Charlotte pull up at the exact same time. Said you two walked together for almost an hour. Everyone knows you never walk, Pastor. Lands, enough times we've seen you running round and round the track at the school like the tax man was chasing you. Not that Lester was watching or anything, but the man's got eyes.

He can't help what he saw. Said you both drove off in the same direction when you were through."

Jock knew better than to protest too much. It would be like throwing lighter fluid on an already glowing grill. He feigned calm.

"Sorry to disappoint you and Lester, but Charlotte and I accidentally ran into each other that day."

"You always run at the school track."

"Overslept that day. Kids were using it."

"Never saw you walk before."

"Pulled a muscle. Getting better, but still hurts when I run."

"Left the same direction. Took the back way."

"Both of us had errands. Believe Charlotte said she had to go by Dr. Ross's for worm medicine for her dogs. I had to go by the tractor place to see Chilly about a donation he wanted to make for the orphans."

Kerilynn's shoulders slumped. "Okay."

"Explain everything to your satisfaction?" He thumped his fingers on the tabletop.

"Nope. There's still one thing."

Jock wondered if he was ever going to get to eat.

"What's wrong with you? Charlotte is the best thing to come to this town. How long's she been here, six months?"

"About that."

"And you honestly haven't thought of asking her out on a date?"

"What I'm thinking of right now is a hot cup of coffee and some eggs."

"Sugar, we've got a little spill over here," called Lucky. "If you'll just tell me where you keep your rags, I think I can clean it up."

"Be right there," Kerilynn replied. She turned back to Jock. "Says in the Bible that it's not good for a man to be alone."

"Says in the Bible that a single person can better devote himself to God," Jock retorted.

Kerilynn went back to her grill.

Jock sat in his tidy office trying to read an article on "Worship Trends for the New Millenium" that contained information about praise teams and drama and something called "worshipful dance." Piece was obviously written by somebody who lived a long way from Ruby Prairie. Some folks here still considered him suspect since he only occasionally used the King James.

God, Pastor Jock believed, was much more concerned with the inside of his worshipers' hearts than the outside. He laid the article aside and prayed, *Lord, help me to focus on what's really important and not get side-tracked. Make my heart right. Help me to lead. Show me Your way.*

When he raised his head, Charlotte Carter came to mind. Kerilynn's words had not come as a surprise. Ever since her move to Ruby Prairie and the discovery that she was single and about his age, matchmaking folks had been scheming.

So why hadn't he taken her out?

She was a new widow.

Not so new. It had been almost a year.

He was her pastor.

Who else better to keep company with than one who shared his same core beliefs?

She had too much on her plate already—six girls, three dogs, two cats.

She had Treasure Evans's help now, and the volunteer ladies and men from the church.

He had no good reason.

Except for one.

He'd told no one, but he was drawn to Charlotte. Too much. Way too much, he believed. Jock found himself looking for her van around town, scanning worshipers to see where she was sitting in church, hoping to run into her at Rick's Grocery Store, the 'Round the Clock, and, yes, the cemetery.

Not since his divorce almost two decades before had Jock been this interested in a woman. Not since his divorce had he dated any woman more than three times. Though he knew he was forgiven of his youthful mistakes, Jock could never shake the memories of the mess he'd made.

What if he was incapable of a relationship? Some people were like the apostle Paul. They should be content to be alone. Maybe he was one of those.

Trouble was, he couldn't get Charlotte out of his mind.

Chapter Seven

Barefoot and still in her pajamas, Maggie strolled into the kitchen. "What's that you're eating?" She poked her finger at the bowl sitting in front of Treasure, who was having a solitary late Saturday morning breakfast.

"Kashi."

"What's that other stuff?" asked Sharita, who had come to see what Maggie was doing. The two had been watching cartoons. Some of the girls were still sleeping. Everyone in the house was enjoying a rare lazy morning, a relaxed few hours during which no one had to be anywhere or do anything.

"Fiber flakes," said Treasure.

"Looks like hamster food," said Sharita. "Why you eating that?"

"Don't you want some pancakes?" asked Donna, in the kitchen to get juice.

"That's what we had," said Maggie.

"With strawberries," added Sharita. "You want some strawberries?"

"Maybe later," said Treasure. "I started my new diet today. Calls for lots of fiber the first week. Don't think I get pancakes until something like Week Five."

"Looks like Week One calls for lots of chewing," said Charlotte, coming into the kitchen. She poured a cup of coffee and sat down at the table.

"You got that right," said Treasure, struggling to swallow a bite. "Maybe I need to let this stuff sit for a while before I eat it." The girls left them alone.

"This diet you've started. New Year's resolution?" asked Charlotte.

"Not exactly. I've been needing to take some pounds off for a while. Figure I need to lose forty, but twenty-five would be a good start."

"Any particular reason you decided to start now?"

"No reason." Treasure took another bite.

Jasper finished painting the fence around his yard, then stood leaning against his mailbox to look over his property. The grand opening was coming up in a week. It had taken some work, but things were looking really nice.

Jasper's place wasn't fancy, but it suited him fine. He'd bought the twenty acres, mostly in pasture, for its location and its view. As soon as he saw it, he knew the property offered the combination of privacy and convenience he was looking for. The house, built in the fifties, was a white frame with three bedrooms, two baths, and a big kitchen. Since he expected frequent visits from his family, the extra rooms would be nice.

The front porch set the house off nicely, as did the black painted shutters and cherry red front door. He'd had to add onto the barn and build horse-suited corrals, but other than that, no major construction had been necessary. Before he'd bought it, and now that he'd settled in, the place seemed to have been built just for him.

Semiretirement so far suited Jasper just fine. All his years of teaching he had opted to live in apartments and little rented places, enabling him most years to put back more than half his salary. Investment income and what he expected to make teaching folks how to ride would allow him to pursue his lifelong passion—horses.

Yep. After years spent teaching rowdy youngsters the basics of agriculture, days of doing what he wanted sounded really good.

What wasn't going quite so well was his adjustment to being alone all the time. Back when he was teaching, he'd had constant contact with his students and fellow teachers. Some days way more contact than he would have liked. Rural retirement, with its long hours of solitude, was going to take some getting used to. Maybe today he'd go have lunch in town.

Jasper looked at the calendar on his watch. In a couple of weeks his house would be full. His relatives were coming to see his new place, and he looked forward to showing it off.

He sure hoped his riding school went over well. If the venture was a bust he could be okay, just might have to think of some other little side job to do. His ad in the *Penny Saver* had generated a few calls from interested folks, and he took that as a good sign. Most callers asked about his hours and his rates, then said they'd get back to him.

That woman Kerilynn at the cafe, the one who said she was the mayor, had assured him that there'd be a big crowd come Saturday. He hoped so. How many hot dogs should he have ready? Should he have chili and cheese for the dogs, or would mustard and relish be enough?

He put out feed for the horses. Belle, as usual, was the first one to the trough. Treasure Evans, his first paying student, had done well on Belle. Been nervous, of course. Short as she was, she'd had a little trouble learning how to mount. Tight pants had made it worse. But Treasure, as she'd told him to call her, had listened and followed every instruction he'd given her. By the end of the hour lesson she had relaxed and enjoyed herself.

Which, as he'd told her, was the whole idea.

Seeing as how Treasure had been his first ever student, he'd given her a discount: twelve lessons for the price of ten. Tuesdays and Fridays were the days they'd set. If she stuck with it, and he bet she would, by the end of the twelve, she'd be well on her way. Today was Saturday. Three more days and he'd see her again.

How would this thing with Beth turn out? Charlotte wrestled over and over with the possibility that Beth might really leave. *Try not to think about it. Focus on today. What's supposed to happen is what will happen. Don't be selfish. Tanglewood might not be the right place for Beth.*

Charlotte was in the kitchen when she got the call from Kim.

Lord, help me to accept whatever comes about. Help me to be happy if Beth gets in. Forgive me for wanting what's best for me and not for her.

"I have news," said Kim.

Charlotte's stomach did a flip. "Yes?"

"Beth got in. She got into Wings of Gold."

71

Charlotte could hear the excitement in Kim's voice.

"Listen to this. One hundred and forty kids were nominated. Only fifty-seven got in."

"So this means?" asked Charlotte.

"It means there's a lot to do in the next ten days. I'll make all the travel arrangements. Beth'll need some warmer clothes. I'll overnight you a voucher. She has to take her own bedding and things for her room—same as if she were going off to college. Of course, there's paperwork to be filled out, medical and dental, and her school records will have to be sent."

A little sob came from Charlotte's throat. "When should I tell her?"

"Now. I mean today for sure," said Kim. "You've got those pictures and brochures that I left for you last time, right? You should show her those."

Charlotte blew her nose.

"Charlotte, listen to me," said Kim. "This is good news. Wings of Gold is an opportunity unlike anything else. She'll get a private school education at no cost. They have mentors there, one faculty member for every five kids. Classes are small. Dance and drama and music are all available and top notch. There's tutoring for every student who needs it. And best of all—if she completes the program, she'll have a college education paid for by the Wings of Gold foundation. Do you know what that can mean in the life of a kid like Beth? In the foster care system, once she's eighteen she's on her own as far as the state is concerned. Imagine being eighteen, and suddenly you're expected to support yourself for the rest of your life without any help or backing from anyone else. Beth will have real support, financial and otherwise. I can't tell you how happy I am that she got in."

Charlotte had to be happy too.

And she was. Even though her heart hurt at the thought of Beth, who'd been through so much, being uprooted again—for even the best of reasons.

"Okay. I'll tell her. Tonight."

"Good. I'll call you tomorrow."

Charlotte hung up the phone.

"Who was that?" Treasure, out of breath from her morning walk, stumbled in through the back kitchen door.

"Kim."

"And?" Treasure sipped cold water from a glass.

"Beth got in."

Treasure plopped down on a kitchen chair, pulled a washcloth from her bra, and began wiping sweat from her brow. "I knew this was coming, but it still hits hard. I don't know whether to cry or be happy. When does she leave?"

"In a week and a half."

"I've gone and gotten attached to that girl."

"Me too."

"If it wasn't for her running away, making you realize you couldn't run this place by yourself, I wouldn't be here," said Treasure.

Charlotte rested her chin in her hands. "I know it's a wonderful opportunity, but I can't shake the feeling that this is not a good time for Beth to be moving. She's been through so much."

"She has," agreed Treasure.

"And I'm still not sure her ankle is completely healed," said Charlotte.

Treasure put her hand on Charlotte's hand. "You know, sugar, we can think up all the excuses in the world, but this is out of our hands."

Charlotte nodded.

"Lord's got His eyes on you and on this house and on ever' one of the girls what you've got under this roof. He'll make it all right. You know it. We've got to believe. When you going to tell her about all this?"

"This afternoon. Soon as she gets home from school. It's not right to wait," said Charlotte. "I thought you could look after the others while I take her for a drive or something. I don't want to upset the other girls."

"Kim coming?"

"Not till day after tomorrow."

"So you've got to break the news to her all on your own." Treasure got up to get herself some fruit. "There's no telling how she's going to take it. I think you need someone else to be with you."

"Who?" Kerilynn was a good friend and would do anything for Charlotte and the girls. So would Nomie or Ginger, but none of the three seemed to be the right person to call on for something like this.

"Call Pastor," said Treasure.

"Jock?"

"Yes. He's the perfect person to be with you when

74

you tell Beth she's going to be leaving. You know his number?"

Treasure was right. Jock was the right person to call.

"I'll start praying about it right now," he told Charlotte. "Why don't you bring Beth here, to my office? And Charlotte—just so you know, I'll be praying not just for Beth, but for you, too."

Treasure and Charlotte studied the Wings of Gold brochure. "Is it a church-run place?" asked Treasure.

"Yes. Well, sort of. Kim said it's run by a nondenominational hoard. The students don't have to be Christians, but they're required to go to chapel every day. All of the faculty are supposed to be believers."

"Sure looks to be a pretty place. You ever been to Colorado?"

"No. Have you?"

"Went there on my honeymoon when I was Beth's age. I still remember. Those mountains—they were the most beautiful things I'd ever seen."

"You got married when you were *fifteen?*"

"I sure did. Forged my daddy's signature."

"How long were you married?"

"Just over seventeen years."

"Goodness. That's a long time to be together and then break up. Were some of those years happy ones?"

"Well, sure. I'd say most of them were. At first I was just tickled pink to be out of my no-account daddy's house. To have somebody to talk to me, to pay attention to me instead of ignoring me day in and day out."

"I don't mean to be nosy, Treasure, but what happened? Why did you get divorced?"

"Oh, honey, it's complicated. Truth is we made lots of mistakes. Both of us. We raised our two girls, then got sort of lazy. I suppose in the end it was our selfishness what killed our love. We each got into the habit of putting ourself first instead of looking out for each other. When I look back, I thank the Lord for forgiving me for my failings, but I still see lots to regret."

"What happened to your husband? Did he ever remarry?"

"He did. To my cousin Acacia. A real sweet girl. She's good to Curtis, and it sounds like he's good to her. Last I heard—the girls keep me up—the two of them were living in a pretty blue house next to some beach in Florida."

"I'm sorry," said Charlotte.

"Don't be. Everything I've been through in my life has brought me to where I am right now. Here. With you and these precious girls. I wouldn't trade being here at Tanglewood for anything in the world." She fiddled with the Wings of Gold brochure. "How are you figuring on telling Beth?"

"Telling me what?" Beth stood in the doorway to the kitchen, still wearing her backpack. Behind her, the other girls were streaming in. As they did on many days when the weather was nice, the girls had walked the six blocks home from school.

Charlotte and Treasure froze.

76

"Hey, there. I didn't hear you come in. How was school?" Charlotte ignored Beth's question.

"Bet y'all are hungry as usual. How about some crackers and milk?" Treasure got up and began pulling snacks from the pantry. "Tell me what?" Beth repeated. "What's wrong?"

Charlotte drew Beth to her and spoke in her ear. "Nothing's wrong, but you and I do have something we need to talk about. Soon as everybody gets a snack, we'll have some time to ourselves. Okay?"

Beth didn't answer. Instead, she turned and ran up the stairs to her room.

Chapter Eight

Beth lay across her bed. She could not stop crying. She had known something was up. Charlotte was mad at her.

But what had she done? She couldn't think of anything. She chewed on a fingernail and tried to go over everything that had happened in the past three days.

There was that argument she'd had with Maggie about what to watch on TV. Was that it? Or the book she'd returned to the school library too late. What about that supper Charlotte made last night? It wasn't very good, and she hadn't eaten much. Maybe Charlotte was mad about that.

Whatever it was that she'd done, she was sorry. Really sorry. When was Charlotte going to tell her what it was? Having to wait wasn't right. How could a person fix what they'd done wrong if they didn't even know what it was?

There was a knock on her door. Before Beth could answer, Charlotte came right in and sat down on the bed. "Beth—I'm sorry you overheard me talking to Treasure. It's okay."

"You're mad at me, and I don't know why." Beth's voice was muffled by her pillow.

Charlotte reached out and touched her arm. "Mad? I'm not mad at all. Why would I be mad at you?"

"I don't know."

"You haven't done anything wrong. Come on. Sit up and look at me."

Beth sat up and wiped her eyes.

"You're not in trouble, Beth. It's something good I need to talk to you about. A surprise."

Charlotte's face didn't look like she had a good surprise. "What is it?"

"You'll find out soon. I want Pastor Jock to be with me when I tell you. Go wash your face, and we'll drive over to his office right now."

"What's Beth in trouble for?" asked Maggie after Beth and Charlotte drove off.

"She's not in trouble. Whatever gave you that idea?" asked Treasure.

Maggie rolled her eyes at the other four girls, but none of them spoke. Instead they got quiet. And busy. All of them quickly became absorbed in their homework, their snacks, their library books.

"What's the matter with y'all?" asked Treasure. "You look like somebody around here has died."

They didn't answer.

They weren't stupid.

Something was wrong.

Charlotte and Treasure were snoring in their downstairs beds. The girls upstairs were supposed to be asleep, but all six of them, along with Visa the cat and Peaches, Treasure's dog, were piled up on Beth's bed.

"Do you really have to leave?" asked Nikki.

"How come?" asked Vikki.

"It's supposed to be a really good school. Kim says I'm lucky," said Beth.

"Do you want to go?" asked Donna.

Beth picked at a loose thread on her quilt. "At first I didn't. Now I sort of do. I don't know."

"I'm not going to be here forever," said Maggie. "Soon as my mama gets out of jail, she's going to come get me."

"When our mama gets well, we're going back home to live with her," said Vikki.

"When my dad saves up enough money, we're going to Oregon to live," said Donna.

"Y'all are lucky. I'll be here till I graduate. All because of those stupid gangs where I live," said Sharita. "I wish you had to stay here as long as me. If you ask me, it's not fair."

"I heard Charlotte say you have to get a whole lot of new clothes," said Maggie.

"We're going to the mall," said Beth.

"I never get to go anywhere," said Sharita.

"I bet you'll get to go up in that helicopter," said Maggie. "You've got everyone in our class coming to church with you, which I think is cheating. Just because I was sick and had to stay home from school the first day after Pastor Jock told us about Friendship Sunday, you got to all of our friends first."

"Yep. You're right." Sharita bounced up and down on the bed. "I'm going to win. But don't worry. I'll wave to all of you when I'm way up there in the sky."

"Don't you get to take someone else up when you go?" asked Donna.

"Pick me! Pick me!" said Maggie.

"Can't. It has to be Charlotte. Pastor said if a kid wins they have to take an adult up with them."

"I'm almost an adult," said Maggie.

"You are not," said Nikki.

"Y'all," said Beth. "I'm kind of tired." Visa was asleep in her lap. "I think we can take the hint," said Sharita.

"Good night."

"Sleep tight."

"Don't let the bedbugs bite."

"Or the fleas," said Sharita.

One by one, the girls went back to their beds. Only Donna lagged behind after the others were gone. "I'm going to miss you," she said.

"Thanks. I'm going to miss everybody here too. Will you write me a letter?"

80

"Sure. And Charlotte's got e-mail. Will you have a computer?"

"I don't know. Maybe."

"Are you scared?"

"A little."

"Are you excited?"

"I really am. I mean, I feel all mixed up. I don't want to leave. I've been in a whole bunch of placements, and Tanglewood is pretty good. But I'm lucky to get to go to this program. You know how in school they always talk about how everybody needs to go to college so they can get a good job?"

"I guess so."

"Well, since I was about in the fifth grade, every time I would hear a teacher talk about that I'd start to worry about what I was going to do. When you're eighteen, the state doesn't give you a place to stay anymore. And they for sure don't help you go to college. But Kim says that if I make good grades and do everything I'm supposed to do, the people at Wings of Gold will send me to college."

"Wow. I guess you are lucky."

Beth was beginning to think that for the very first time in her life, maybe she was.

Kim couldn't wait until Monday to check back with Charlotte. She called Sunday morning, even though it was her day off.

"Did you tell her? How did she take it? Is she excited? Upset? What did she say?"

"She's still kind of in shock. At first she didn't say much of anything. Then she told me she didn't want to leave."

"I'm not surprised."

"But we talked some more. It was one of the hardest things I've ever had to do—selling her on the idea of going into the Wings of Gold program. But you know, by the time we were through talking about it, I'd about convinced myself that it's a good thing."

"Wonderful! You know, Charlotte, that it actually is a good thing."

"Beth had a lot of questions. Some I couldn't answer."

"That's okay. Jot them down, and when I come I'll do my best. And if I don't know something, we'll call Beth's contact person. Her name's Cheryl Armey. How did the other girls take the news?"

"The twins cried. Sharita got mad. Maggie sulled up. Donna started saying her stomach hurt."

"The thought of Beth leaving is bound to stir up some of their issues," said Kim. "Tell you what. Don't the girls have the day off from school on Wednesday? I'll plan on spending the day at Tanglewood. That way I can spend some time with each of them one on one."

After her lesson, Jasper asked Treasure to come inside for a cup of coffee and some cake. The coffee she took, the cake she declined. She was down three pounds and not wanting to undo the good that she'd done.

Jasper's house was nice. Plain, as you'd expect a

bachelor's house to be, but clean. He didn't have many decorations except for a few dozen framed pictures he'd hung all the way down the center hall.

"Who are all these folks?" Treasure asked.

"Family." He proceeded to tell her the names of them all. His parents and his grandparents. A couple of aunts and a trio of uncles. His daddy was gone, but his mother was still living. He had a brother, Royce, and a sister, Harriet, both of whom had spouses, children, and grandchildren, all of whom he was as proud of as if they were his own.

"Are you close to them?" Treasure asked.

That brought a chuckle. "Let's just say I've got plenty of folks who make it their business to stay in my business. Course I let 'em. I'm the baby of the family. My brother and especially my sister think that it's their job to see that I keep myself on track."

"Do you see them often?"

"Several times a year. Matter of fact, they're all coming here the first weekend in February. Having a family reunion right here. Harriet can't stand it that I went and bought this property without her having laid eyes on it!"

"First weekend in February? The sixth?"

"Believe so."

"Why, that'll be Friendship Sunday at Lighted Way," said Treasure. At her invitation Jasper had already visited the church twice.

"You don't say. Well, I reckon I'll be doing my part to shore up the attendance that day. Probably won't make it to Sunday school. It takes my aunts longer to get themselves ready than it takes ice cream to freeze. You don't reckon a few dozen extra black folks will upset any of the good members, do you?"

"Aw, you know how it goes. I imagine there's some who'd rather none of us were there, but they keep their thoughts to themselves. No one has been anything but kind to me since I first started coming."

"Is there a black church in town?"

Treasure raised one eyebrow. "You seen many black people running up and down the streets of Ruby Prairie?"

"Not to speak of."

"That's prob'ly why there's no black church."

"Does it bother you? Being in a town that's mostly white?"

"Some. Have to drive a half hour to get my hair done, is the worst thing. Ladies say Lila here's good, but she don't know the first thing about my hair. And she doesn't carry the right line of products. And Pastor Jock. He's as good a man as I've ever met, but sometimes the services are a little, uh, sedate, I guess you could call it."

Jasper snorted. "Yep. No offense, but I'd go along with that."

"I still like it here," said Treasure, surprised that Jasper's comments made her feel defensive. "Town's full of good people. The church folks aim to serve and praise the Lord; they just do it in their own way. As for me, I came here to help Charlotte out for a few weeks.

I ended up liking it so much I decided to stay on."

"How'd you know Charlotte?" asked Jasper.

Treasure told Jasper about the kindness Charlotte's grandmother had bestowed on her so many years before. "Charlotte's a good person. Just like her grandma was. I love her just like I love my own two girls."

"Where do they live?"

"One's overseas. Her husband's in the service. The other one lives in Florida. I don't get to see either of them nearly enough."

Jasper nodded. "I guess not."

"What about you? What brought you to Ruby Prairie?"

"Always wanted to live in East Texas. I love the trees. Weather's not bad. I don't mind the heat. I'd been looking for the right piece of property for the last few years. Price of this one was right. I bought it, and here I am."

"Here you are." Treasure pushed her coffee mug back.

A long moment passed, during which neither of them said a word. "You coming to the grand opening on Saturday?" It was Jasper who finally spoke.

"Wouldn't miss it. Bringing five of Charlotte's girls. She's been thinking some of them might like to learn to ride."

"Thought you said there were six girls at Tanglewood."

"One's leaving. Got accepted into a private school."

"I suppose running a home like that, a person gets used to kids coming and going," said Jasper. "I reckon you have to keep yourself from getting too attached."

"No way to keep from it," said Treasure. "And Charlotte doesn't even try. She told me one time that her goal is to treat every one of the girls in her care as if they were going to be with her for the rest of their lives. Of course she's only had her home since last fall. This one, Beth, is the first one to actually leave."

"Sounds like setting yourself up for lots of heartache."

"It's going to be hard on all of us, but we're happy for the child. She's blessed to get accepted into this program. It'll see her through college. Believe Pastor Jock's planning on a bit of a send-off for her on Friendship Sunday."

On Saturday Charlotte and Beth took off for the mall, a good hour and a half away. They went in Treasure's old two-seater van, leaving Charlotte's big one for Treasure to take the rest of the girls to the grand opening of Jasper Jones's Riding School.

"Do we get to ride a horse?" asked Nikki.

"Probably. Imagine it depends on how many folks show up. You'll have to take turns," said Treasure.

"Is there going to be food?" asked Maggie.

"Hot dogs. But didn't you just eat breakfast?" It was only ten o'clock.

"Yes. Four pancakes. I'm not hungry yet. I was just asking for later."

Charlotte and Beth stopped for a late breakfast at IHOP. Beth ordered chocolate chip pancakes, Charlotte, French toast.

"What'll you have to drink, young lady?" the waitress asked Beth.

"Orange juice."

She wrote that down, then turned her attention to Charlotte. "And for you, Mom?"

Charlotte stumbled over her words. "Um, coffee. With uh, cream. And a glass of water."

"Coming right up."

After the waitress had gone, Charlotte fiddled with her napkin, then finally spoke. "I couldn't be any prouder of you if you were my daughter, Beth. I'm going to miss you. More than you. know. But I am so happy for you."

Beth's eyes misted over. "Part of me is so excited I don't know what to do. The other part of me wishes everything could stay the same. I like Tanglewood. I can't believe I ever ran away. How could I have been so stupid?"

"Every one of us does things we regret. Me included. I'm sorry you ran away. I'm sorry you broke your foot. But look at how, things have turned out. You've changed. You've grown up. Isn't it amazing how God can take the worst of us and make it into something good?"

"I want to be a good person," said Beth. "I want to make up for—" She swallowed. "I want to make up for all that other stuff."

"Hard, isn't it?" said Charlotte. "No matter how much

we try, we never feel good enough. You and I have talked about this before, remember? When you were in the hospital after the surgery on your foot? Honey, God loves you more than you can imagine. No matter what you do. If you forget everything else I've ever said, I want you to remember this. There's nothing you can do to make Him love you more. Nothing you will ever do or have ever done can make Him love you less. You are His precious child."

She reached over and covered Beth's hand with her own. "And you are my precious child too. I know I'm not your mother. She should be the one sitting across from you instead of me. You've not known me long, but I am making this promise to you. Even when you leave to go to school, I'll be here for you. Holidays, Tanglewood is still your home. When things aren't going well, or you just feel lonely, you call me. I love you. Your leaving Tanglewood doesn't change that."

"I don't know what to say." Beth had trouble meeting Charlotte's gaze.

"You don't have to say anything. End of sermon. Let's enjoy our breakfast. Then it'll be time for a little retail therapy."

"Retail what?"

"Shopping!"

Chapter Nine

Someone was pounding on Jasper Jones's front door.

It was an hour and a half before the grand opening

was scheduled to start. Jasper, soapy, barefoot, dripping, and damp in hastily pulled-on jeans and a shirt, was mortified to open his door and find Ruby Prairie's mayor standing on his front porch.

It didn't appear to bother her a bit.

"I am so sorry. You want to come in? Just give me a minute. I'll be right out."

"Why, don't mind me. You go on with what you're doing," said Kerilynn. "Your property looks really nice, Mr. Jones. Jasper, isn't it? Who painted your sign? It's wonderful. My, my, would you look at this sunshine? Couldn't have ordered up a better day. Tell you what. I'll be outside making myself useful. Anyplace special you want me to tie the balloons?"

Balloons? Jasper hadn't known he was having balloons. "Uh, no. Anywhere's fine. Anywhere you see fit." What else had she brought that he didn't know about?

From ten until twelve—those were the hours he'd put in the paper and printed on the information sheets he'd left at the 'Round the Clock. At least that's what he thought he'd put. Maybe he'd gotten it wrong.

"Anywhere'll be fine. Anywhere you think they'll look good. I appreciate you bringing them. I sure do."

"Bless your heart," said Kerilynn. "You're standing here not even dried off. Go on back and finish your bath, Mr. Jones. I've got lots to do to get things set up."

Jasper Jones closed his front door and padded back to the bathroom, where he stripped off and got back under the hot water. *Get things set up?* He'd mowed the grass, bought hot dogs and fixings, and made lemonade and iced tea. Hay bales were set out so folks would have a place to sit while they ate. When it was closer to the time folks should show up, he planned to saddle all six of his horses so everyone could see how they looked. Then, he hoped, they'd maybe pick out a horse they'd like to learn to ride, and sign up for a series of six or twelve lessons.

That was his plan.

Wonder what "lots to do" it was the mayor was talking about?

Fifteen minutes later, dressed in pressed Wrangler jeans, a crisp white pearl-snap shirt, and polished cowboy boots, Jasper came out his front door. Not yet nine o'clock, but another vehicle was parked next to the mayor's station wagon in his circle driveway. Balloon clusters of red, white, and blue were tied to the fenceposts that ran up to his house. How had she gotten all those done so fast? And who else was here?

"Hello there."

It was the pastor from Lighted Way Church getting out of his pickup truck.

"I know we're early, but a couple of the members and I decided to come on a little ahead of time in case you're needing any help."

As Pastor Jock spoke, from around the side of Jasper's house came a short little man. What was he doing around there?

"Lester Collins. Parked around the side." The man offered his hand. "My wife, Ginger, is still in the car.

You don't have any dogs, do you? She's been afraid of dogs since she was a child."

"No. No dogs. A couple of cats, though."

"I love cats," said Ginger, once Lester had told her the coast was clear. She flashed Jasper a smile, then made him nearly lose his balance when she gave him an enthusiastic, unexpected, full-body hug.

Woman had some strength to her. Bit of a surprise, seeing as how low she was to the ground.

"We're so glad to have you move into our community," she said. "Hope you'll be happy here and stay a good long while."

"Sorry we didn't get to meet you last week," said Lester. "We were in Houston. Grandkids had parts in a play at their church. You know how that goes."

Jasper, still unsure why the couple was here, nodded that he did.

"Kerilynn said she got word you planned on cooking your hot dogs on top of the stove," said Lester. "Not one thing wrong with that, but Ginger and I got to thinking. You don't want to be running in and out of your house getting folks food. Half of them'd be apt to follow you inside. Tracking mud and no telling what else on your floors."

Jasper nodded again.

"Pastor came by this morning, and we decided we'd just load my grill up in the back of his truck and bring it on over. Thing's heavy, though. You reckon you could help us unload it? Take a bit to get the coals just right, but once we do, we can cook those dogs outside. Be lots easier on you, and they'll taste better too. Where you want to set up? Under that far tree?"

"That's very generous of you. Thank you. And yes, under that tree will be fine," said Jasper.

"Did you pick up mustard and relish?" asked Ginger.

"Yes, ma'am. Plenty of each," said Jasper. Had she brought that too?

"Chili?"

"No. I thought I'd just—"

"Well, good. I'm glad you didn't get any, because I picked up a case of Wolf Brand last time me and Lester was over at Sam's Club. Don't know why I bought it. We'll never eat all that. Poor Les. Loves chili, but he gets that acid reflux every time he eats it. Stays up most of the night. Anyway, I brought along six cans. If you've got a pan and a can opener, we can set it to heating up on a corner of the grill."

"That's nice of you—" Jasper began.

"Wait till you see what I've brought to do the ribbon cutting with," Kerilynn interrupted. "It's in the backseat of my car. Come and see; then you can show me where it'd be best to set it up."

"Is your house unlocked?" asked Ginger. "'Cause if you don't care, I'll go on in and get your can opener and a pan. Don't worry; I can find it. My grandmother always said that a woman can go into a stranger's kitchen and find something her husband couldn't locate in his own home. Some truth to that."

Jasper didn't know what to do first. Help unload the grill, go into the kitchen and get a pan, or follow Kerilynn to see what exactly it was she had brought.

"Hold on." Pastor Jock met Jasper's eyes. "Mr. Jones, you have to excuse us. Sometimes in our readiness to help, we come on a little strong. Every one of us is glad you are here. We want you to know that. This is *your* grand opening. I'm sure you know what needs to be done and how you want it done. Now, how can we best assist you?"

Kerilynn, Lester, and Ginger all froze where they were. Pastor was right. Thing was, it was easy to get all caught up in the excitement of something like this. They hadn't meant any harm.

Jasper found his feet. "First off, please call me Jasper. None of this Mr. Jones business. Y'all are real nice to come and help me out. I've got one riding student already. Maybe you know her. Treasure Evans? She warned me Ruby Prairie folks were the friendliest and most helpful she had ever met in her life. I can see she's exactly right. Might take a city boy like me some time to get used to, but I can already see I'm going to like it here in Ruby Prairie. Now what say we get that grill unloaded? Under that tree will be fine."

Jasper quickly saw that there had been no need to worry about whether folks would come to his grand opening.

"Folks in Ruby Prairie will show up to watch their neighbor burn his trash if they hear refreshments are being served," Kerilynn had said.

By ten o'clock folks were pouring in, most of whom he'd never seen before, a few of whom he'd met at the cafe or at Lighted Way. "Catfish Martin," said one of the first men to arrive.

Jasper shook his hand. "Pleased to meet you."

"I own the bait shop and video store downtown. It's the one with the American flag in the window, next door to Joe's Eye-talian place. I carry 'bout any kind of bait you want. Snacks too. Mainly cold drinks, cheese crackers, Moon Pies, peanuts, and the like. Got a good selection of movies. Whole section of John Waynes."

"I'll keep that in mind," said Jasper. "Of course since I—"

"Don't be coming in my place looking for any of them dirty movies, though." Catfish didn't let Jasper finish his thought. "I don't keep 'em. If a person's of a mind to pollute hisself with such trash as that, they'll have to carry their business someplace else."

"I don't own a VCR."

"Got one of them DVD players?"

"No. Don't watch much TV either."

Rant interrupted, Catfish changed the subject. He pushed his cap back from his head and looked around. "Nice place you got here. But whew-ey. I hate to think what property taxes are going to run you. Chilly sell you this place?"

"Chilly?"

"Chilly Reed. He's the real estate man around here. Got the tire store out by the interstate."

"Haven't met him."

"Catfish, you are not interrogating this poor man, are you?" Kerilynn, wearing a gray felt cowboy hat and blue jeans, joined them. She turned to Jasper. "I see you've met my twin brother. I know, I know. We don't look nothing alike. I count my blessings every day."

She winked at Jasper so Catfish could see. "Let me tell you. No matter what my brother says to you, don't go paying him any mind. Man's not regular. That's why he's so grumpy all the time."

"Kerilynn!" Catfish turned red in the face.

His sister ignored him. "Lots of folks are here. You and your carrying on are taking up too much of Jasper's time. Let the man go so he can meet everybody."

"Good to get to know you," said Jasper, taking a moment before responding to the mayor's tug on his arm. "You'll be seeing me in your store real soon. Got a pond stocked with catfish on the backside of the property, and I've been itching to drop a hook into that water. Come on out some afternoon when the weather's good, and we'll see what we can pull out of that pond."

Catfish gave Kerilynn a withering look. "Sounds good. I'll do it."

There were lots of folks to meet. Hands to shake. A bunch of names to try and remember.

"I'm Nomie Jenkins. This year's president of the Ruby Prairie Women's Culture Club. On behalf of the club, welcome to Ruby Prairie." She handed him a pie.

"Boots Buck. My wife, Alice."

"Gabe Eden. Volunteer fire chief. Wife, Rose Ann, couldn't make it. She's a nurse. Works every other weekend at the rest home. You've probably seen it, way out on the north end of Main."

"New Energy?" asked Jasper.

"That's it. You ought to go on down there and take a look at the place. Them old folks love to have company, and the food's not bad either. You can go out there and eat lunch, long as you call ahead and tell them you're coming."

Jasper had wondered what the place was. New Energy. And it was a rest home?

"I'm Lila Peterson." A pretty young woman shook his hand. She pointed to the corral where Jasper had saddled and tied up the horses. "Those two blondes, the ones climbing up on your fence, are my daughters, Jessica and Jamie. They're both crazy for horses. Been pestering me something terrible to get them one. First it was a trampoline, then one of those above-ground swimming pools. Lands. We sure don't have room for a horse. But before I leave I'll be signing them both up for lessons. Do you give a discount for families with more than one child?"

Jasper allowed that he did. Before moving to the next person waiting to meet him, he promised Lila he would make her a good deal.

"Hello. Thank you for coming," said Jasper to a man with black hair and dark eyes.

"Welcome to town. I am Joe Fazoli. I have restaurant in town. You come in. I give you free dessert your first time."

"Thank you. That's very generous," said Jasper.

He spotted a familiar face, Dr. Lee Ross, Ruby Prairie's veterinarian. "Good to see you, Dr. Ross."

"Everything looks really nice. Your mares are looking good. How's that gelding doing? The one that was lame?"

"Fine. See him? Tied up on the end. He's doing great," answered Jasper. "He limped around for a couple of days, then got over it."

"I expected as much, but glad to hear it. You've had a good turnout." At the sound of a vehicle's engine, the two of them turned to see who was pulling up.

"Believe that's Treasure Evans. Bet she's brought the Tanglewood girls," said Dr. Ross. "You know about Charlotte Carter and the home she runs for troubled kids?"

"Yes. I've heard about it." Jasper had been wondering where Treasure was. "Actually, Treasure was my first pupil. Doing really well."

"That right?" asked Dr. Ross. "Good woman, she is. A big help to Charlotte. Loves those girls. Looks to me like she's brought a bunch with her. Bet you'll have some takers if you let the children ride."

It was right about then that Mayor Kerilynn decided it was a good time to get down to business. "Okay if I ring the bell, Jasper?" she asked.

Jasper loved the big old antique dinner bell. It was mounted on a set-into-the-ground decorative pole just to the side of his back door. His guess was that in years past it had been used to call workers in from the back forty for lunch. He'd spotted the bell when he looked at the property and made sure it was written into the contract that it would stay.

"Sure," he said. "That'll get everyone's attention, for sure."

Kerilynn pulled on the rope. Everyone stopped their conversations and began gathering around.

"Folks," she said, "we're here today to welcome Mr. Jasper Jones to our community and to help him get his new business started off right. Sure glad you've all come. Wouldn't be a grand opening without a ribbon cutting. But since our regular ribbon didn't seem exactly fitting for a horse farm, I brought something a little bit different." She pulled from her satchel a length of new rope. "Where are Jessica and Jamie? Those girls of Lila's said they'd help me out."

The girls came, and Kerilynn gave one end of the rope to each and told them where to stand. "Now, Jasper, why don't you come on up? Say a few words, and then do us the honors." She handed him a pair of garden clippers, then whispered in his ear, "No way would a pair of scissors cut through that. Take you all day."

Jasper cleared his throat. "I'm not much for speaking to crowds. Mainly what I want to say is thank you all for coming. I'm happy to be a part of the community. If I can be of assistance to any of you, please let me know. There's hot dogs and chili for everyone to enjoy. If any of you are interested in signing up to learn to ride, I'd be happy to quote you my rates and to set you up a time. I suppose that's about it. Pastor—" he scanned the crowd for Jock—"once I've cut this rope, could you offer a blessing for the food?"

"Terrible waste, cutting a new rope clean in two like that," Catfish said under his breath, but loudly enough for everyone to hear. "Shush," said Kerilynn.

The crowd parted, and Pastor Jock stepped forward. He put his hand on Jasper's shoulder and bowed his head to pray. "Father, thank You for bringing Jasper Jones our way. May his life here be happy and his business be prosperous. May he be a blessing to us, and may we be a blessing to him. Thank You for the food we are about to eat. In Jesus' name. Amen."

"And amen," echoed the crowd.

"Grill's hot. Got plenty," called Lester from his cooking spot under the tree.

"Y'all can have hot dogs," said Treasure to her charges, "but not before you show some manners. Come on up here. You need to meet Mr. Jones. Be nice now. Smile at him and thank him for serving us this good food."

Ginger was just then asking Jasper if he'd gotten any napkins. Hearing Treasure's voice over Ginger's head, Jasper caught her eye, flashed her a smile, and waved her and her bunch of girls forward.

"I want to pet a horse," said Nikki.

"Not me," said Sharita. "They stink." She held her nose.

"Stop that," said Treasure. "Be polite."

"They're really pretty," said Donna. "I like the tan one."

Treasure finally maneuvered her crew to where they could meet Jasper.

"Good to see y'all," he said. "Treasure's told me all about you. Anybody here want to ride today?"

Everyone did, even Sharita, who declared that maybe the horses didn't smell so bad after all.

"Come on, girls, y'all can come too," Jasper called to Jessica and Jamie. "Careful now," he said. He opened the gate and led the girls inside the corral.

"First off, I'm going to introduce you to Honey. She's one of my gentlest mares. Now, don't ever walk too close behind a horse. Sometimes they kick. Talk nice and easy to her. Reach out your hand slowly. That's it."

Transfixed, one by one the girls touched Honey on her neck.

"Horses are like people. You come up on them too quick like or speak to them too sharp, they'll spook on you. They need time to decide you're not something to be scared of. Y'all can understand that."

Treasure's girls nodded.

Yes. They could understand that.

Pastor Jock and Treasure sat on hay bales eating hot dogs. Jasper had given each of the girls a short ride. He'd held the reins and led Honey around inside the fence. He was now inside the barn, going over his schedule book, signing folks up for lessons.

"Charlotte busy this morning?" Pastor Jock asked.

"Gone shopping with Beth. Getting her the things she needs for when she goes to Colorado."

"Is Beth excited?"

"Getting that way. Hates to leave Tanglewood.

100

Excited about where it is she's going. Child's been moved so many times, I reckon saying good-bye for her is not the same as it would be for me or for you."

"How's Charlotte doing?"

"Better than I thought. Girl's got a heart of gold. She just wants what's best for Beth. Her getting into that school is an answer to prayer, even if her going breaks all of our hearts."

"God doesn't always answer our requests in ways we expect," said Jock.

"You can say that again," said Treasure. "I'm living proof of that."

Chapter Ten

Donna was setting the table, Nikki and Vikki were pouring glasses of water and milk, and Treasure was ladling up bowls of chicken and dumplings when Charlotte and Beth, carrying six shopping bags between them, came in through the kitchen door.

"You're home!" said Treasure. "And just in time. Lands, did you two girls leave anything in the stores for anybody else?"

"We want to see," said Donna.

"What took you so long?" asked Vikki.

"I never get anything new," said Sharita.

"We went to the grand opening, and Mr. Jones let us ride a horse," said Nikki.

"Can we take lessons?" asked Maggie.

Charlotte and Beth crossed the kitchen to drop their

packages at the bottom of the entry hall stairs.

"Sounds like we've all had an exciting day," said Charlotte. She gave them hugs. "I want to hear all about the grand opening; just give me a minute to take off my coat. I'm starving. That smells so good."

"Where's Beth?" asked Donna.

"She went to the bathroom," said Sharita.

"Soon as she gets back, let's have some supper. You can tell us about the horses. When we're done, Beth can show you her new things."

Beth's bedside digital clock said 12:15. She knew she should be asleep. Tomorrow was Sunday, and everyone had to be up early to get ready for church. Though she'd put on her pajamas and brushed her teeth, she couldn't make herself get into bed. Instead, she arranged and rearranged her purchases. Never in her life had she had so many new things.

There was a heavy coat, boots, a hat, and gloves and a scarf for weather colder than any she'd experienced in the temperate climate of Ruby Prairie. Charlotte had insisted on buying her new socks and underwear, enough that when added to what she already had she could go ten days without having to do laundry. She'd also purchased jeans and sweaters, cotton turtlenecks, and a couple of skirts. Their last acquisitions had been items for Beth's room at school: sheets and a comforter, pillows, curtains, and a bright throw for the end of her bed.

It felt weird showing the other girls all the new stuff.

102

Only Sharita said anything, and since she was always going off about something, nobody paid her any mind. But how could they help but feel sort of jealous, with her getting so many new things, getting asked to the new school? And their being left behind?

She and Charlotte had talked about it a little on the way home.

"I'm not used to being the lucky one," Beth said. "I've always been the one people felt sorry for. Over and over I'd have to move because something went wrong in my foster home. People would feel sorry for me. My caseworker, my friends—if I'd been there long enough to make any friends—my teachers, sometimes even the foster parents. They would all look at me like I was some poor little orphan or something. I hated that."

"I bet you did." Charlotte looked over at her, but kept both her hands on the wheel.

"The whole time I just wanted to be like everyone else. Normal. You know? But sometimes I wondered what it would be like to be one of those kids who got all the breaks. The smart kid who wins the spelling bee, or the popular girl who gets elected president of the class, or the one person in the state who gets their American history essay chosen to be read to the governor. That happened to a girl who sat behind me when I was in fifth grade. I used to look at people like Aubrey and wonder what it would feel like to be special like them, to have everyone wish they were you."

"So how does it feel?" said Charlotte.

"Like I'm dreaming, and maybe I'll wake up and it won't be true."

"The countdown's on," said Kerilynn at the 'Round the Clock.

"What are you talking about?" asked Nomie and Sassy. They'd come in for Kerilynn's liver-and-onions Monday lunch special.

Kerilynn put extra on their plates. She knew for a fact that neither of them cooked much for themselves anymore.

She filled the ladies' iced tea glasses, brought them extra rolls, then tossed her dish towel over her shoulder and pulled up a chair. "Friendship Sunday in six more days. Then Charlotte's girl Beth leaves for Colorado two days after that."

"I, for one, don't know about all this helicopter business," said Sassy. "Are those things safe? Seems like you hear about them crashing all the time."

"I don't know if they're safe or not, but they sure do have the children in my Sunday school class worked up," said Nomie. "Every one of them is determined to bring the most visitors and win the ride. I won't be surprised if the Baptists and Methodists just call off their services and come on over to ours."

"Whoever's in charge of feeding the flock had best be counting on an extra big herd," said Sassy.

"That would be me," said Kerilynn. She got up and came back with three pieces of still-warm-from-the-oven homemade coconut meringue pie.

"I thought Boots was making chili," said Sassy.

"He is," said Kerilynn. "And Lester's doing his fried peach pies. I'm not cooking; I'm organizing. Got to see that there's enough paperware, make the tea and the coffee, get tables and chairs set up in the fellowship hall. When it's all over, I get to see that it's all cleaned up and everything put back where it goes."

"You'd have gotten off easier if you'd signed up to do all the cooking yourself," said Sassy. "Come Sunday, it'll be Boots and Lester taking all the credit, but you'll be the one too tired to move."

"Some things never change," said Kerilynn. "Y'all want coffee with your pie?"

Pastor Jock, spotting both Treasure's and Charlotte's vans in Tanglewood's drive, decided this would be a good time to stop by. He was careful not to call on women, single or married, when they were home alone.

"Why, it's the pastor." Treasure opened up the front door. "Come in. You're just in time for some lunch."

He stepped inside.

"Charlotte, you've got company," she called over her shoulder. "Pastor Jock's come to see you."

"Actually, I came to see both—"

"Wait right here." Treasure left him standing in the entry hall.

"Maybe this isn't a good time?" called Jock. He heard Treasure whispering, then Charlotte whispering something back. He looked at his watch. Eleven forty-five? How did it get to be nearly noon? He hadn't meant to show up right at mealtime.

"Sure it is," said Treasure, reappearing. "Perfect time, that is. Come on in the kitchen and pull your coat off. You want a glass of iced tea?"

"Thank you. But no, I won't be staying long."

Charlotte rounded the corner from the direction of her downstairs bedroom and bath. "Well, hello! So good to see you, Pastor. Treasure and I were just about to sit down for lunch. Stay and eat with us."

"You like taco soup?" said Treasure. "It's left over from last night, but soup's always better the second day."

"I didn't stop by to get fed," said Pastor Jock.

"Like we're supposed to believe that." Treasure winked at Charlotte. "I've never known a preacher who wasn't good at showing up just in time to eat. Figured that was something they taught you fellows in seminary. Set yourself down."

Jock shook his head. "All right. You've gone and twisted my arm."

"Speaking of twisting, when my cousin Shirley was younger, she loved to cook for folks more'n anybody I've ever seen. When you sat with your feet under Shirley's table, you were going to eat some of ever' thing she fixed, two or three helpings, whether you wanted it or not. Then she'd start you on dessert. Her grown son told me one time that if there wasn't nobody around for his mama to cook for, she'd stir up something for the cat. 'Ever' hour she feeds that cat,' he told me. 'If it won't eat, she twists its tail.'"

"Sweet or unsweet?" asked Charlotte, after she'd

filled Jock's glass with ice.

"Cheese? Cornbread?" Treasure fixed his plate.

"I'm fine with just soup. Really. Don't go to any trouble." He hadn't intended to come into these women's house and have them wait on him hand and foot.

Treasure gave him a look.

"Okay. Yes. Some of both."

"Butter on your cornbread?" Treasure pointed to a chair at the table, motioned for him to sit down.

"That would be great."

Finally Treasure and Charlotte joined him at Tanglewood's round oak table. At Charlotte's bidding, Jock gave thanks for the food.

"This lunch is a treat. But mooching a free meal is not what I had in mind when I rang your bell. I want to talk to you about doing something special for Beth at Sunday's service. I think it would be nice to give her a going-away blessing."

"I'm not sure." Charlotte stirred her soup. "I don't know how Beth would feel about that kind of attention, especially if she had to stand up in front of people at church. She's still embarrassed about running away. She's had a hard time getting over knowing that folks were talking about her."

"Talk or no talk, everyone at Lighted Way loves Beth. Remember how hard they prayed for her when she was gone? Lots of folks think of themselves as being in a small way responsible for the wonderful turn her life's about to take."

"They are responsible," said Charlotte. "And not just

for Beth. Without the help of so many kind and loving people, Tanglewood would not still be open, and these girls would not have this home."

"Then let them give Beth a blessing before she goes," answered Jock. "I'm not talking about some kind of big production. I was thinking of offering special prayers for her at the end of the service, then maybe presenting her with a Bible inscribed from Lighted Way Church."

"Might be a nice touch if everyone stood up and sang 'Till We Meet Again,'" said Treasure. "We could hold hands."

Jock nodded. "Excellent idea. We do the same sort of thing in the spring for the young people who are graduating from high school. I'd like for Beth to come and stand up at the front, but if she'd prefer to stay in her seat, that's fine too."

"It won't take away from Friendship Sunday, will it?" asked Charlotte.

"Not a bit. Honestly, Friendship Sunday is just one day of the year when members are encouraged to invite guests to come to worship with them. Sure, we have a meal afterwards, but other than that it's the same as a regular worship service."

"Regular Sunday, my foot," said Treasure. "I don't recall seeing a helicopter on the lawn every other Sunday of the year."

"Don't remind me." Pastor Jock grinned. "That was not any of my doing."

After Jock was gone, Treasure and Charlotte carried

their dishes to the sink. "Nice man," said Treasure.

"He's a very good pastor," said Charlotte.

"Good looking too," said Treasure. "That sweater he had on fit him like a glove."

"Did it?" said Charlotte. She focused her concentration on the sink full of soapy water. "I didn't notice."

"You didn't?" said Treasure.

"Nope," said Charlotte. "And by the way, I don't know why you sent me to the bathroom to comb my hair. It looked fine to me."

"I was trying to do you a favor. You don't think it's a good idea for a single woman like yourself to freshen up a bit when she has a gentleman caller?"

Charlotte ran more hot water in the sink. "Pastor Jock didn't come by on a social call, and I was not in need of any, as you say, freshening up."

"You saying you're not interested in the man?"

"No."

"Not at all?" Treasure stood leaning on the counter, her hand on her hip.

"Not at all."

"Okay, I think I see now. You've got no interest in him, so you had no reason to do any primping on his account."

"That's right."

Treasure wet a dishcloth and began to wipe the table. Charlotte dried her hands on a clean towel. "Think I'll run to the store. We're out of milk. Anything else we need?"

"Not that I can think of."

Charlotte slung her purse over her shoulder and turned to go. "By the way," Treasure addressed Charlotte's back. "I like that cologne you've got on."

Charlotte's neck turned red.

"Guess you just happened to put a little dab on when you went back to run that comb through your hair. Nice touch."

Chapter Eleven

The week flew by. Pastor Jock worked on his sermon. Kerilynn concentrated on procuring enough disposable bowls, paper plates, napkins, and cups to feed the expected army. Lester made last-minute preparations for cooking up his famous fried peach pies. Boots, helped by Alice, premixed the spices that would go into his chili and put them into ziplock bags. Two bags he labeled "Two Alarm," one he labeled "False Alarm."

"Going to make up two pots of hot and one pot of mild," he told Kerilynn.

"Good idea. Kids probably won't eat the hot. Some of the older folks what have that acid reflux'll appreciate it too. I've got all the paper goods. Lila Peterson's supplying the crackers. Nomie and Catfish said they'd bring grated cheese. You think of anything I've forgot?"

"Just plenty of iced tea. You know my two-alarm pots'll be plenty hot.

On Friday afternoon Charlotte arrived at school thirty minutes before the dismissal bell. Kim had told her she needed to get Beth's records for Wings of Gold. Miss

Evans, the office secretary, took her request, then disappeared to a back room.

"So you're checking Beth out." Ben Jackson, principal of Ruby Prairie School and fellow member at Lighted Way, saw Charlotte standing at the counter and came out of his glass-walled office to say hello.

"She leaves on Tuesday."

He motioned Charlotte into his office. "Miss Evans'll have to make copies. Why don't you take a seat while you wait."

Charlotte sank into a chair opposite Ben's desk. The last time she'd been in this office was before she'd taken her first girl. She'd come to let the principal know of her plan to turn Tanglewood into a home for troubled girls.

She'd been impressed then with Ben's kindness and warmth. When she'd heard he was young—only thirty, with no wife or children of his own—she'd worried he might not be empathetic to girls who could cause problems for the school. Thankfully, her fears had been unfounded. Ben had been nothing but supportive and helpful.

"I know she'll do really well," he said. "Beth's a good student. According to her test scores, she falls into the gifted student category. Her past school records don't indicate that, but bless her heart, she's been on more than half a dozen campuses in three different states. It's a wonder she even learned to read."

"Do you know much about Wings of Gold?" asked Charlotte.

"I heard the school's founder speak at a conference a couple of years ago. He grew up poor, the child of an absent father and an alcoholic mother. An anonymous donor, someone whose name he never learned, sent this man to college, and after that to grad school. Today the school's run by a board and financed by individual-donations, grants, and money from charitable founda-tions, but he still oversees the whole operation. His mission is to assist promising students the same way his benefactor helped him."

"Kim told me that only a few students are accepted. Beth's getting in was a shock to everyone," said Char-lotte.

"It's a wonderful opportunity for her . . . but I imagine it must be hard for you to see her go. Will you be get-ting another girl once she leaves?"

Charlotte hadn't even thought of that. The bell sig-naling the end of the school day interrupted their con-versation. Then Miss Evans returned with a sealed folder.

"Just need you to sign right here before you leave, Miz Carter," she said. "You'll let us know how Beth gets along, I hope."

"Yes, ma'am," said Charlotte. "I will." She turned back to Ben. "Thanks for telling me about the founder. That helps."

The secretary left the room as the hall outside began to fill with noisy students.

Charlotte moved to go, but Ben cleared his throat. "Just a second," he said.

She turned.

"I know now's not a good time, but once things settle down a little for you, after Beth leaves and everything, would you like to have dinner sometime? I mean, would you like to have dinner with me?"

So caught off guard was Charlotte that before she knew what was happening, she'd told him yes.

Minutes later, she was still so rattled by the exchange that, her van loaded with Tanglewood girls, she pulled out of the school parking lot and headed the wrong way down the one-way street.

Treasure Evans folded her paper napkin into a tidy, two-by-two-inch square, unfolded it, then folded it again. "Thank you for the coffee." She glanced at the clock over Jasper's kitchen sink. "I enjoyed today's lesson."

"You're coming along really well," he replied. "And the coffee's my pleasure. You sure you won't have another cup?"

Treasure shook her head. "Charlotte'll be getting home with the girls about now. They'll have a snack, but in another hour or so the whole bunch of them'll be starving for their suppers. I need to be on my way."

"I've got to take care of my batch of hungry critters too. Gone and got them all spoiled. They expect their suppers right on time."

Neither of them made a move to get up. Instead they sat peering at their reflections in their coffee mugs.

"You got plans this weekend?" asked Jasper.

Treasure's heart did a little flip. "A few. Be helping Charlotte get Beth packed up, I suppose. Of course there's Friendship Sunday. This is your reunion weekend, right?"

"Yup. Expecting at least ten of them, could be a couple more. You know how it is with young people. They don't know themselves what they're doing one minute to the next."

"Doesn't sound like Pastor Jock needs to worry about a good attendance come Sunday. Your family alone will fill up a whole pew."

By Saturday afternoon thirty-three relatives had descended upon Jasper Jones's house. He was totally surprised at the number, glad for his full freezer, and thankful for the extra paper goods he had laid in.

"Beautiful place you've got here, Son," said his mother, soon as she was helped from the car. "Just wish you weren't off so far away, is all."

Jasper hugged his mother's neck as she wiped at her eyes. His great-nieces and -nephews, free of the confines of car seats and seat belts, tumbled out of minivans like reckless puppies.

"Can we go see the horses, Uncle Jasper?" they asked.

"Sure you can. Long as you don't go inside the fence."

"This is the best turnout we've ever had for a Jones reunion," said Auntie May.

"Which way to the bathroom?" asked Auntie June.

"Where you want us to put all our stuff?" asked his brother, Royce.

114

"Food in the kitchen. Everything else in the back room. We can sort it out later," said his take-charge sister, Harriet.

Jasper's relatives did not come empty-handed. They brought with them food, gifts for his new house, camp cots, sleeping bags, extra blankets and towels, and church clothes.

The service was over. Pastor Jock had done a really fine job with his sermon, everyone agreed. The turnout was a good one, it looked like, though the official count had yet to be announced. Pastor Jock offered a prayer for the food, and folks were sitting down, enjoying their chili, hoping for seconds on Lester's peach pies.

Jasper was thankful for the welcoming words Lighted Way members expressed to his family. He had a hunch some of the older members had never seen this many black people in one place, though by their friendliness, no one would have ever known.

"Everyone is real nice here, Son," his mother whispered just before Gabe got up to speak.

Gabe called for everyone's attention. "First off, I'd like to say a big thank-you to everyone who helped make this Friendship Sunday a success. Kerilynn, for organizing everything, Boots for cooking the chili, and Lester for providing his pies. Other folks stayed behind the scenes, but they put in lots of work none of us'll ever know about. If you're one of those folks, the Lord knows who you are. We thank you and count on Him to bless you. And thanks to Pastor for that good lesson he brought us. I say let's give them all a big round of applause."

"When is he going to say who won the contest?" whispered Sharita loudly. "I brought ten visitors. No way anybody else brought that many."

"Where's the helicopter?" asked Maggie. "I thought somebody was going to get to take a ride."

"I'm gonna be mad if I won and there ain't no helicopter." Sharita folded her arms across her chest.

"Shhh," hissed Charlotte. "Both of you. Be quiet."

It was right about then that a buzzing sound interrupted Gabe's speech. It grew louder and louder, till he gave up trying to talk over it. Loose windowpanes in the fellowship hall began to rattle. Babies began to cry.

"Lands," said Jasper's mother. "Is that some kind of a bomb?"

"I believe our helicopter has arrived," yelled Gabe, grinning ear to ear. When the noise seemed as if it couldn't get any louder without tearing the roof off the church, the engine shut off and it was quiet again.

Everyone looked expectantly at Gabe, who in turn watched the back door. Within seconds, the door opened and the pilot walked in.

"Welcome," said Gabe. "Welcome to Lighted Way. Appreciate you coming."

The pilot, sleek in a navy blue jumpsuit, nodded and gave the crowd a wave.

"Kerilynn," said Gabe, "how about you fix this man a bowl of chili? You hungry, sir?"

The man nodded, and Kerilynn motioned him to

follow her into the kitchen.

"While he's having some lunch," said Gabe, "Pastor's asked me to let everyone know that today's attendance has broken all prior Friendship Sunday records. We had a total of 227 in attendance today. That's wonderful. We want all you visitors to know you're welcome to come back and see us anytime. This is a loving church. A church on the move, as we shall soon see."

People began to fidget. Most had finished their meal. But Gabe wasn't through.

"I know you're all wondering who brought the most visitors. Am I right about that, young people?"

"Yes!" chorused the group.

"Think you're going to be surprised," said Gabe. "Are you ready?"

"Yes!"

"You really, really want to know?"

"Yes!"

"This year's winner, the person who brought the most visitors, the person who will get to take a ride in the helicopter is—" He paused for dramatic effect.

"Tell us! Who?" said Maggie.

"Jasper Jones!"

It was at that exact time that Jasper bit into one of Lester's fried pies, causing the hot peach filling to squirt out and burn the roof of his mouth.

"Come on up here, Mr. Jones," said Gabe. "Some of us have met your guests, but many of us haven't yet had the honor."

Jasper made his way to the front. "I appreciate this.

117

Really I do, but I'm not even a member of this church. I expect I'll be joining, but as of today, I'm a visitor here myself. It wouldn't be right to claim the prize."

Gabe scratched his head, then looked to Pastor Jock for a cue. Pastor Jock joined Gabe at the front. "Jasper, we're so proud to have you and your family here with us today. We hope that after putting it to prayer you will see fit to join our church. In the meantime, who was it that invited you to be with us today?"

Jasper didn't hesitate. "Why, Treasure Evans. She invited me when we first met and kept reminding me all week that I ought to come today."

"Then that settles it," said Jock. "Treasure, we're crediting to you Jasper Jones and all of his family. You're the person who's brought the most visitors today, and you're the one who'll be taking a ride over our fair city."

"No fair!" said Maggie.

"If that don't beat all," said Treasure, shock showing all over her face.

"Thank goodness," said Charlotte under her breath. "I just knew Maggie would win and I'd have to go up. I don't think I could have done it."

Ben Jackson was seated across the table from her. "You're not scared of heights, are you?" he asked.

"You have no idea."

Gabe had more to say. "Treasure Evans, come on up here. Congratulations! You ever been up in a helicopter before?"

"No, but I've always wanted to," she said.

"Wonderful. Today's your day. Question is this. You know that whoever won today gets to take another person along for the ride. Have you given any thought as to who that might be?"

"I have."

"Me! Me!" said Maggie.

"That's not fair!" said Sharita.

"I've always wanted to take a helicopter ride," said Donna. "How are you going to choose between all of these girls?" asked Gabe.

"I'm not," said Treasure. "I'm asking Jasper Jones to join me on this ride. Seems only fair, since it was him and his family that got me this honor."

The crowd broke into applause—everyone but the Tanglewood girls.

"Jasper? You up for this?" asked Gabe.

Jasper rose to his feet. "You bet. I'd like to get a bird's-eye view of this town."

"Son! Are you sure?" said his mother.

"Didn't the Lord say 'Low I am with you always'?" quipped Royce.

"I'd be honored to take a ride with this lovely lady," said Jasper.

The pilot had finished his chili and was waiting at the back. When Gabe caught his eye, he nodded his readiness to go.

"All right, then. Let's step outside and see these two off."

Jasper got in first, then he reached for Treasure and helped her up the step. Once inside, his face only inches from hers, he flashed her a kid's grin. "Thanks for asking me. When I was a boy, a man at the county fair was selling helicopter rides for fifteen dollars. Might as well have been a million, it was so out of reach."

The pilot helped them get buckled in. His seat was in front, theirs side by side in the rear. "All set?" he asked.

"You bet," said Jasper, not one bit afraid.

"I think so," whispered Treasure.

"You nervous?" asked Jasper.

"Just a bit."

At that he took her hand. Held it, for the very first time.

When the engine started, the noise was so loud that it allowed no more talking. Quickly, they were off the ground. Higher and higher they rose until they could see the roof of Lighted Way Church, then the length of the street that ran in front of it, and finally the entire town.

Jasper could see Treasure's fear. Her hand was cold and damp in his. A surge of protectiveness washed over him. He straightened a bit in his seat, sat up a little taller. It was good she'd chosen him to join her on this ride. Woman needed someone to make her feel secure, help calm her nerves. He doubted anyone else in the church would have had the same effect. Him teaching her how to ride a horse had set her up to feel safe with him.

He patted her hand and mouthed the words, "You okay?" Shaky, she nodded.

"You're going to be fine," assured Jasper.

And then he threw up.

Chapter Twelve

"I had no idea," said Charlotte. The girls were at the church for youth group. Charlotte and Treasure, worn out from Friendship Sunday activities, had decided to skip evening services just this once. With their shoes off and their feet propped up, they were enjoying the quiet, sipping mugs of tea, both deeply sunk into the over-stuffed chairs in Tanglewood's firelit living room.

"I don't think anyone else knew either," she continued. "But now that I think about it, that helicopter was back down on the ground for a rather long time before the two of you got out. And Jasper sure did gather up his family and leave in a hurry."

Treasure took a too-fast sip, burned her mouth, then nodded. "You got that right. He got out of there quicker than a tick jumping off a flea-dipped dog."

"How in the world did you—you know—get it all cleaned up?"

"Luckily, the pilot had a roll of paper towels and a jug of water. We just did the best that we could. Have to tell you—it was an awful mess."

"I bet Jasper was embarrassed."

"Mortified. I thought the man was going to have a heart attack on top of being sick. For his sake, I hope you're right about folks not knowing what it was that was going on."

"Did he say anything about feeling ill before you took off?" asked Charlotte. "Boots's chili was pretty spicy."

"Not a word. Man nearly worried me to death making sure I was all right. Kept telling me not to be afraid, encouraging me to look out the window, telling me about the pretty view, then—"

"Just like that," said Charlotte. She wrapped an afghan around her cold feet. "This is terrible of me, Treasure, but you have to admit, the whole thing's a little bit funny."

"I know it. Once we got him cleaned up, he looked so miserable. I had to work hard to keep my face straight. Bless his heart. Man may never get over it."

"Maybe you ought to call and see how he's doing," said Charlotte.

"Nope. His family's still here. Some of them aren't leaving until Tuesday. I reckon his mama and his sister are taking good care of him."

"You two seem to be getting along really well." Charlotte sent Treasure a teasing smile. "Seems to me your relationship is a bit more than just teacher and student."

"Maybe," said Treasure. "Maybe not. I'll let you know soon as I've got something to tell. Speaking of which, that young man what runs the school sure was hanging close to you today. How many times did he get himself up to get you more iced tea?"

Charlotte feigned innocence. "You mean Ben Jackson?"

"That's the one. And just so you know, I wasn't the only one that noticed him sniffing around. I saw Pastor Jock noticed it too. Saw him watching the two of you. Don't think he liked it much either." Treasure's glasses slid down her nose, and she looked over them at Charlotte with a challenging gaze.

"Mr. Jackson's interested in Beth, that's all," said Charlotte. "He was asking about her flight, when she was leaving and all."

"Whatever," said Treasure. "Not one thing wrong with the man." She clucked her tongue and pushed her glasses back up on her nose. "Say—are they feeding those girls at the church, or have we got to have them something fixed when they get in?"

"They're feeding them," said Charlotte. "Leftover chili." Treasure groaned.

Later that night, Beth was lying in her bed with Mavis the Tanglewood dog asleep at her feet. Except for its old-house creaks and groans, Tanglewood was still. Through the room's two floor-to-ceiling windows, a clear, white winter moon shone so brightly that the patterns of the window's lace curtains appeared scattered across her pillow. A million thoughts, and one big worry, ran through Beth's head. She tried her best to make it go away. *There's no way,* she told herself for the hundredth time. *Everything's going too good. Stress. It's just stress.*

Charlotte's knock made both Beth and Mavis jump.

"Are you asleep yet?"

"No."

"Okay if I come in?"

"Sure." Beth moved over, and Mavis shifted too.

Charlotte sat down on the bed. She smoothed back

Beth's hair, tucked the covers up around her shoulders, and let out a breath. "Only two more nights here. You think you'll miss this bed?"

"I know I will." Beth turned over on her side, propped her head up on her hand.

"What did you think of Pastor Jock's special prayer for you this morning? Was it okay, or did it feel like too much?"

"At first I was afraid he was going to make me come up to the front and look at everybody. I'm so glad he didn't do that. But it was all right, what he did, telling everyone I was leaving in two days, then saying that prayer."

"That's how I felt. Like he did everything just right," said Charlotte. "Did many people say things to you afterward?"

"Some. Ginger Collins asked me for my address and wrote it down in a little book. When some of the other ladies heard her asking, they wanted it too. I feel bad. I don't even know all their names."

"I wouldn't worry about it. It'll be nice to get some mail. How about tonight at youth group? Was that okay?"

"They asked me a lot of questions about Wings of Gold. They couldn't believe it when I told them there's an indoor swimming pool and a bowling alley right on campus."

"You didn't tell them the bowling alley only has two lanes, did you?" teased Charlotte.

"I guess I left that out." Beth grinned.

124

"Tomorrow, we'll go over all your things, make sure we haven't forgotten anything. If we have to, we'll make a Wal-Mart run. I made an appointment for you at Lila's for two o'clock. I thought you might want to get your hair trimmed before you go."

"Thanks. My bangs are getting sort of long."

"Then tomorrow night, we'll have the first traditional Tanglewood send-off dinner. Eventually, every girl who comes here is going to have a last night. You get to help me decide what special things we do. Any ideas?"

"Could I get to choose what's for dinner?"

"Absolutely. What'll it be?"

"Chicken-fried steak, mashed potatoes, green beans, rolls, and cherry pie."

"Consider it done." The surprise cake Sassy was bringing over would be an extra treat. "What else?"

"I don't know. You think maybe I could get a little present to give to the other girls? Nothing big. Just something they can remember me by?"

"That's a great idea. If we can't find the right thing here in Ruby Prairie, we'll go on to Wal-Mart."

Beth shivered.

"You going to be able to sleep?"

"I don't know," said Beth. "Probably not."

"Me either," said Charlotte. "Are you scared?"

"A little."

"I think that's understandable. Kim says there'll be someone from Wings of Gold, a Mrs. Lambe, if I remember right, who'll meet you at the airport and help you get settled in. Way I understand it, every student has a faculty member assigned to them for the entire time they're at the school. Mrs. Lambe will be your special person until you graduate."

Beth hadn't known that.

"I understand lots of new students are starting right now. Kind of an odd time, I thought, but evidently Wings of Gold isn't on the same schedule as other schools. When I talked to them the other day, they told me your roommate is a new girl too. Someone from way off. Rhode Island, I think."

"You know her name?"

"I wish I did."

The two of them sat in silence for a long moment. Finally Charlotte bent down and kissed Beth on the forehead. "Just wanted to tell you good night. Sweet dreams. See you in the morning."

After she was gone Beth thought of a million things she wished she could say. Why was it so hard? Years of shuffling from foster home to foster home had made some words stick in her throat. Simple words.

Thank you.

I'll miss you.

I love you.

Please don't forget me.

I'll never, ever forget you.

Words like that. They always got stuck.

Beth was the only girl still in her pajamas.

"How come we have to go to school and Beth don't?" asked Sharita.

"Not fair," said Maggie.

"I don't want to go to school either," said Nikki.

Charlotte plopped hot, brown-sugared oatmeal into eight bowls while Treasure buttered toast. If this bunch didn't get their cranky selves in gear, the whole lot of them would be late.

"Beth's not going because I've already done the school paperwork to have her withdrawn," said Charlotte. "We've got to finish packing her things. She has to get a haircut. Some of her laundry needs to be done. We have to have everything ready for her to leave tomorrow."

Donna, who'd come down the stairs just in time to hear Charlotte's last words, dropped her backpack on the floor, slumped into a chair, and started to cry.

"What's the matter?" asked Charlotte.

"I don't know. Everything's messed up," said Donna.

"Something's always wrong with her," said Sharita.

Donna raised her head and shot Sharita a dirty look.

Right then, Vikki knocked over her glass of milk. Icy cold, it ran off the table and into Maggie's lap, prompting her to jump up and shout a forbidden word.

"Maggie!" Treasure sopped up the milk with a rag.

"I hate oatmeal," said Nikki.

"We have it every day. I hate it too," said Vikki.

Treasure burned a batch of toast.

Nikki, standing at the refrigerator, announced that there was no more milk.

"I hate this place," said Donna. "I wish my dad would come and get me and take me to live with him."

The entire Tanglewood crew was headed for a melt-down. Charlotte should have seen it coming, but in the midst of all the packing and preparations, she had missed the signs. Still standing over the oatmeal, she shot up an SOS of a prayer.

God, help me know what to say to these girls. They're upset. I guess I'm upset too. Lord, truth is, we're all upset. Give me wisdom. Calm this house down. Thank You. Amen.

"Okay. Up from the table. Everybody to the living room. Now."

Grudgingly, they trooped behind her, took seats on the sofas and on the floor. Only Beth chose not to sit down. She stood in the doorway, arms wrapped around herself. Not until Donna scooted over and motioned for her to join her on the love seat did she sit down.

Charlotte took a deep breath. "Everybody's upset. It's more than getting up on the wrong side of the bed, isn't it? Tell me. What's everybody feeling?"

No one in the room met her eyes.

Finally Donna spoke. "I don't want Beth to leave."

"Me either," said Maggie.

"Why does she have to go to that dumb school anyway?" said Maggie.

"What's wrong with our school?" asked Nikki.

Treasure spoke up. "We've talked about this. Y'all know that Beth's getting to go away is a blessing from God. I think what's wrong is you girls feeling bad about your own selves."

"It's hard to be left behind. To watch someone leave,"

said Charlotte. "There's nothing wrong with feeling sad or mad or unhappy. I'm feeling all of that myself. But you girls need to tell me or Treasure what's going on. We can't read your minds."

"That's right." Treasure nodded.

"Okay," said Charlotte. "Let's just go around the room. I want each one of you to tell me what's on your mind. Who wants to start? Maggie?"

"Wait. I want to go first," said Sharita.

"She always goes first," said Vikki.

"What I wanna know," said Sharita, "is who gets to sleep with Mavis when Beth leaves? I think it should be me and nobody else."

It was past ten before the girls had gotten things talked out, eaten their rewarmed oatmeal, and dressed for school. Treasure loaded them all in the van and headed out.

Not until they were gone did Beth have the bathroom to herself. "You going to shower now?" Charlotte called up the stairs. "Yes. I'm about to get in," Beth called back.

"Soon as you're ready, we'll head to Lila's."

"Okay."

Alone in her room, Beth retrieved the box from where she'd hidden it under her bed. She'd had it for a week, thought every day about using it, but kept putting it off. Just one more day, one more day, she'd told herself. She'd bought the kit while on a school field trip. After visiting two art museums, the students had been

129

allowed two free hours at the mall, which fortunately had a drugstore.

Beth held the box in her hands. *Thank You.* God had to have worked that out.

Surely He could work this out too.

She closed herself up in the bathroom and turned on the shower so Charlotte would hear it running, and whispered another prayer.

Please God. Please let it be okay.

Was that a bad thing to pray? Probably.

For about the five hundreth time Beth prayed again. *God, I'm sorry. Please forgive me. Make it be okay and I promise, I promise I'll never, ever, ever do it again.*

Then she sat down on the toilet, opened the box, and spread its contents out on the counter beside her.

Charlotte dressed in a hurry. Her last day with Beth. How would she get through it? She prayed while she brushed her teeth.

God, I'm going to miss her so much. I know it's a blessing she's going, but how am I going to get through this?

She reached for the floss. Empty. Add that to the growing list of things to pick up while they were out shopping. Charlotte tried to skip flossing. Silly, but she couldn't. Not flossing would bother her all day. The girls had extra. She'd snag a piece from their upstairs bathroom.

Through the closed bathroom door, Charlotte heard water running. Shoot. Beth was still in the shower.

Maybe she hadn't locked the door. "Beth, honey," Charlotte said as she turned the knob. "It's just me. I need to get some—"

She didn't finish her thought.

Beth, still in her pajamas, was standing at the bathroom counter, staring down at a small plastic tray indented with two little side-by-side white circles. In each of the circles was a bright pink plus sign.

"Beth," Charlotte whispered. "What are you doing?"

But she already knew the answer.

Chapter Thirteen

How could this be? Charlotte, like Beth, couldn't take her eyes off the test. Her thoughts raced. Her heart pounded. Then she began to cough from the steam.

A low wail came from Beth's throat. She sank to the tile floor, ducked her head, drew her knees to her chin, and began to sob.

Charlotte turned off the shower, then joined her on the floor.

The animal-like cries that came from Beth were the most anguished sounds Charlotte had ever heard. Tears filled her own eyes as she gathered the lanky teen in her arms and held her as tightly as one would a hurting young child.

Beth didn't pull away, but she seemed not to even feel Charlotte there.

For more than an hour Charlotte held her in her lap. For more than an hour, Beth continued to weep. Charlotte could not catch even a glimpse of her face. Occasionally her sobs would slow down, only to start up again even harder than before.

Charlotte did not let go. She didn't talk. She didn't stroke or caress. She simply held tight.

It was close to noon when Charlotte felt Beth's body relax just a bit. She reached up and wiped at her nose with her sleeve. Charlotte loosened her hold, and Beth eased herself away from Charlotte's embrace.

"What's going to happen to me?" she whispered.

"I don't know, honey," said Charlotte. "I think we'd better call Kim."

"This changes everything," said Kim. "First, she needs to see a doctor. The sooner the better. Let me see if I can get her in today. I'll call you right back."

Charlotte paced downstairs while Beth took a shower. Finally the phone rang.

"Beth's got an appointment with Dr. Lovington at two o'clock," said Kim. "He'll be doing a sonogram to determine exactly how far along she is and to make sure the baby's okay."

The baby. Beth was having a baby. The words did not sound right.

"Where is his office?" asked Charlotte.

"Dallas."

At least an hour's drive.

"There's a doctor in Ella Louise. That's only twenty minutes away. She can't go there?"

"No. Because of her age, and the X-rays and drugs

132

they gave her when she was in the hospital, she's considered high risk." Charlotte hadn't thought of that.

"Are you coming up?"

"I'll be at the doctor's office in time for her appointment, but I won't see you before."

"Does the doctor she's seeing know the situation?"

"Some of it."

Charlotte's stomach churned. *God, please let him be kind.* She could hear Beth moving around upstairs. *Oh God. Oh God.*

That was all she could pray.

Treasure bustled in the front door just as Charlotte hung up the phone. "You look like somebody just told you your dog went and died. Those girls," she continued, "they was still fighting and picking at each other when I made them get out and go in. Lands. I don't know what we're going to do with them."

Only after she'd taken off her coat and hung it up in the hall closet did she look into Charlotte's pale face, see her red eyes. "Uh-oh. What's happened?"

Charlotte shook her head. Put her finger to her lips. She couldn't speak. When she turned toward her bedroom, Treasure followed.

Charlotte motioned for her to close the door, and Treasure came to sit next to her on the bed.

"You torn up over that child leaving?"

"She's not. Beth's not leaving," said Charlotte.

"What do you mean? Of course she is. You've done real good with all of this. I know it's been hard, but you've got to be strong, do what's best by her."

"Treasure. Beth's pregnant."

"What are you talking about? I've only been gone an hour. Would have been back sooner, but—What do you mean, Beth's pregnant?"

"I walked in on her. Upstairs in the bathroom. She had one of those home pregnancy tests."

"Oh, Jesus, no. Please. Don't let it be so. . . . You think the test could be wrong?"

"She says she hasn't had a period since she's been here."

"Why, that's more than three months," said Treasure.

"Four," corrected Charlotte.

"Four months! You mean—"

"She's got an appointment with the doctor. We've got to leave right away to get there in time. We'll know more after she sees him."

"Bless that child's heart. How long do you think she's known?"

"I don't know. She's not saying much, and I didn't ask many questions."

"How could she let this go on and not say anything to anybody?" Treasure wrung her hands.

"She was scared. She's fifteen years old. She was in denial."

"I never saw any signs," said Treasure.

"I took her shopping last week. We bought her new *underwear*," said Charlotte. "How could I not have noticed *something*?"

"Sometimes young girls don't show for a long time,"

said Treasure. "I don't recall her being sick to her stomach."

"Me either. I've been trying to think back. She did seem really tired when she first got out of the hospital. Remember how she went to bed early, before any of the other girls, for a week or so?"

From outside the door, all three of Tanglewood's dogs began to bark. "Lands," said Treasure. "Somebody's here."

Charlotte wiped her eyes and blew her nose. She pushed aside the curtain to see whose car was in the drive. "It's Pastor Jock."

"Lord's spoken to his heart this morning," whispered Treasure. "Timing's perfect. Sent that man to this house so as to pray with you, that's what He did. You go wash your face. I'm going to let him in."

"Hi, Jock." He was still standing in the entry hall when Charlotte came out of her room.

"Morning," he said. "I know Beth's leaving tomorrow. Thought I'd stop by, see if there's anything I can do to help out."

Charlotte, who'd stopped crying, now started again.

It was Treasure who spoke first. "Pastor, we've had some terrible news this morning. Beth's not going to that school. She's staying right here."

Charlotte found her voice. "Beth's pregnant."

"Oh, no," said Jock.

Charlotte shook her head. "Oh, yes."

"I'll pray," he said. "I give you my word that I'll pray."

135

Charlotte went to get Beth from her room. She was dressed, had on her socks but not her shoes. Even from across the room, Charlotte could smell her hair. Freshly washed but still slightly damp. When she moved, the scent of lavender wafted Charlotte's way. Beth's favorite. It was what she'd requested and what Charlotte had purchased for her to take to school.

Beth had made her bed. The room, while always tidy, was even neater than usual this morning, cleared of all her packed-up personal items. Placed against the wall between the two floor-to-ceiling windows was a small tote bag and Beth's backpack. Both were stuffed full and zipped. At the end of the bed her new footlocker, a gift from Lighted Way church members, stood open, revealing neat stacks of clothing, linens, and books.

"Is Kim coming?" Beth asked in a small voice.

Charlotte looked at her watch. "Not right now, but we'll see her at the doctor's office. She's made you an appointment. I'm really sorry, honey, but we have to leave in just a few minutes—actually right now—to make it in time."

"I have to go to the doctor?"

"Yes. It's really important. For you. And for the baby. He'll do an examination."

Beth looked stricken. "You mean I'll have to take off my clothes?" Charlotte nodded.

And Beth began to cry again.

Chapter Fourteen

Dr. Lovington turned out not to be a he. Slim, fair skinned, and with a wild mop of strawberry blonde curls, she was more than what Charlotte had prayed for her to be—kind, compassionate, gentle, even a bit funny. She looked young, and a big diamond ring sparkled on her left hand. Pictures of babies and children decorated the walls of the exam room.

Charlotte stayed with Beth, standing discreetly near her shoulder while Dr. Lovington did the pelvic exam. For the first time she glimpsed the telltale bulge of Beth's sure-enough, confirmed-by-the-doctor pregnancy. This was real. She had harbored the faint if unrealistic hope that maybe somehow this was all a mistake.

Charlotte's palm and fingers went briefly to her own lower belly. Her body, like Beth's, had once sheltered life. Unbidden, thoughts of that pregnancy, the only one she and her late husband had ever managed to achieve, came into her mind. Memories of the joys of that pregnancy, chased by the thoughts of the sadness of the miscarriage, overtook her, fresh and sharp after all these years.

"Try to relax," said Dr. Lovington.

Beth gripped Charlotte's hand.

"This may be uncomfortable, but it shouldn't hurt. Do you know when you had your last period?"

"I don't remember." Beth's eyes were squeezed shut.

"Are they regular? Do they come at the same time every month?"

"No."

"Okay. Almost done." Dr. Lovington helped Beth to sit up. "I'll step out while you get dressed; then I'll come back and we'll talk. After that, we'll do a sonogram. I think you're about four months. From the sonogram we'll know more. Okay?"

Four months? Charlotte reeled. That meant Beth had indeed been pregnant the entire time she was at Tanglewood. She *had* to have known. Quick anger shifted to feelings of compassion. How alone Beth must have felt. How afraid. No wonder she had kept so much to herself. No wonder she'd seemed depressed. The child had not known what to do.

Charlotte pretended to read a magazine while Beth, back turned, got dressed. They didn't talk. Shortly after Beth had taken her seat in the chair next to Charlotte, there was a knock on the door. Dr. Lovington's receptionist peeked in.

"Kim Beeson is here. Says she's Beth's caseworker? Is it okay if she comes back?"

"Yes. It's fine," said Charlotte.

"I'll just show you into the doctor's office, so there'll be room for all of you to sit."

When Kim came into the office, she spoke to Charlotte first. "I'm sorry I'm late." Then her eyes found Beth.

Beth looked up at Kim, then looked back down.

Sensing her embarrassment and hesitancy, Kim

moved first. She pulled Beth into a long, wordless hug. "You doing okay?"

Beth nodded.

"We're okay," said Charlotte.

When Dr. Lovington returned, Kim introduced herself.

The doctor seated herself behind her desk and spoke directly to Beth. "You're fifteen. But you're not a child, and I'm not going to treat you like one. You are in a very adult situation. With this adult situation come responsibilities. Choices. There are decisions that have to be made. By you, Beth. Not by anyone else. I'm here to support you, to give you information and options, and to answer your questions. You have Charlotte and Kim here as well. But as far as I'm concerned, you are in charge. Do you understand?"

Charlotte shifted in her seat.

"You, Beth, must decide what you want to do about this pregnancy. And soon. Do you understand what I'm saying?"

Charlotte did not like the way this conversation was going. She opened her mouth to speak, but Beth cut her off, speaking her first full sentence since their arrival. "I'm not having an abortion, if that's what you're talking about. I'm not doing it."

Dr. Lovington looked at Charlotte, then at Kim, and finally back at Beth, who met her gaze without even a blink.

"All right then." Dr. Lovington made a short note on Beth's chart, then closed it. "This lets me know how to proceed." She paused, then spoke her next words slowly, carefully. "I agree with your decision. I have never, nor will I ever take the life of a child. But not everyone feels as I do. And there are risks, both to Beth and to the baby. It's important that you know."

No one said anything in response.

"I'm sure you'll have lots of questions as the pregnancy proceeds. I'll be seeing Beth every two weeks for a while. As you think of things, write them down. Before you leave today, my nurse will show you a video and give you some booklets to read. As for right now, let's do the sonogram. Ready to take a look?"

Dr. Lovington's nurse led them to the sonogram room and helped Beth lie back. "No need to get all undressed," she said. "Just unzip your jeans and lower them a bit. That's right. Good. Dr. Lovington will be right in."

"You may think we keep this jelly stuff in the fridge, but I promise we don't," said Dr. Lovington. "I'm going to squirt some onto your belly, and it's going to feel really cold. Then I'll move this little gizmo around so we can see what we've got."

Back and forth across Beth's tummy, Dr. Lovington moved the imaging tool. Every few seconds she would stop, and the machine would make a clicking sound. "Baby's first pictures," she explained.

At first Beth kept her eyes closed. Charlotte held her hand. Was she planning not to look at all? She was impossible to read. On the drive over she had looked out the window and chewed on her nails before falling asleep the last thirty minutes.

"You sure you don't want to see?" asked the doctor. "It's pretty cool. Not gross at all."

Beth opened her eyes. Maybe she'd thought she'd see blood. Once her eyes adjusted to the screen, her gaze, like Charlotte's, was transfixed on the screen.

"Just as I thought. Looks like you're right at sixteen weeks." Dr. Lovington kept moving the wand. Back and forth. Up and down. "All the organs appear to be developing as they should be. Major vessels are in the right place. Placenta looks good. I'm afraid the way the baby's positioned, I can't tell the sex. It would be a bit early even if we could see. Questions?"

Beth shook her head.

Dr. Lovington used a tissue to wipe off the goo, then helped Beth sit up. She placed her hand on Beth's shoulder. "I know this was hard. You are a very brave girl. You can go with the nurse now, and I'll see you in two weeks."

"Call if you have any problems before your next appointment," called the receptionist a little later as the three of them headed out the door.

Outside in the sunshine, Charlotte looked to Kim for her cue as to what to do next.

"The three of us need to talk," said Kim. She turned to Charlotte. "You remember where my office is?"

"I think so. But drive slowly, and I'll follow you."

In the car, Beth buckled up. Her face stoic, she kept her eyes focused straight ahead. It was not until they pulled up in front of the ugly gray government building that she spoke in a flat little voice. "Kim's going to say I have to go someplace else, isn't she?"

"Is that what you think?"

Beth nodded.

"No. She's not." Charlotte turned off the key and turned in her seat to face Beth. "Not if I have any say, and I believe that I have a lot. As far as I'm concerned, you have a home at Tanglewood. Your being pregnant doesn't change that. Unless you want to go somewhere else?"

"I want to stay. It's just that now that you know that—"

"That you're not perfect?" Charlotte interrupted. "That you've made some bad choices? Honey, I knew that way before all this, and I wanted you then. I still want you now. My commitment to you has nothing to do with what you've done or not done."

"I'm so sorry." Beth bit her lip. "And I'm so embarrassed. What about the other girls? What's Treasure going to do when she finds out? What about my teachers and school and everybody at church?"

"They'll have to know. We have to tell the other girls. Today. It won't be long before most every person in town will hear the news. You know how it is in Ruby Prairie. Some folks won't understand. Some of them will."

She looked up and saw Kim standing at the entrance to the building, waiting for them. It was time to go in.

"Come on. Let's hear what Kim has to say. You and I will talk more on the way home."

It was nearly five o'clock before Charlotte and Beth

left Kim's office. Charlotte phoned Treasure on her cell phone.

"I been praying every minute since you left," said Treasure. "I thought you'd be home by now. Is Beth all right? Are you all right?"

"Everything's okay. It's been a long day, but Beth's going to be fine. Unless we hit traffic, we'll be home in about an hour. I was thinking—why don't you take the girls to Joe's for dinner? Wait about forty-five minutes, then head out. That way Beth and I'll come home to a quiet house. It'll be much easier to be at home waiting for the girls than to have to face them the minute we walk in. By the time you and the girls get back home, we'll be there."

"Well, sure, I'll carry them down to Joe's. But, Charlotte, when you planning on telling them? You can't keep this from them for long."

"Tonight, when you all get back from eating. I agree. It can't wait. They're expecting her to leave for Colorado tomorrow."

"Maggie and Sharita have been talking about moving their stuff into her room."

"Those two. I'm not surprised. I'm sorry, Treasure. I know you're in a bad place. If you can just placate them for another couple of hours—"

"No problem. I can handle these girls. You just bring yourself and that one what you've got with you back home safe. It breaks my heart the mess she's done got herself into, but I have to be honest: It was breaking my heart to send her off like we was. Leastwise now we get to keep her."

"We'll see you in a bit, then," said Charlotte, about to hang up. "Wait, one more thing."

"What's that?" asked Treasure.

"Pray, okay?"

"Honey, I haven't quit praying all day."

Charlotte ended the call.

"You heard all that?" she said to Beth. "No one will be at the house when we get there. At least for a half hour or so."

"Do I have to be the one to tell them?" asked Beth.

"Not if you don't want to," said Charlotte. "I can do it."

"I don't know how to tell them. How would I say it? How am I going to face them? What are they going to say? Are they going to be mad?"

Nothing worked out according to plan. Joe's was closed, so Treasure ended up feeding the girls tomato soup and grilled cheese at home. Charlotte and Beth could see them at the table when they drove up.

As soon as they stepped into the light of the entry hall, Nikki and Vikki sprang from their places at the table to give Charlotte hugs. Treasure, right behind them, pulled Beth into her arms and kissed her cheek before she let her go.

"What took you so long?" asked Nikki.

"I thought you were getting your hair cut," said Vikki. "It looks the same to me."

"Come on back to the table, you two. Finish your

supper. Let Charlotte and Beth catch their breath. You two eat yet?"

Beth headed to the bathroom, Charlotte to the kitchen, where the others were still eating. She willed her face to be calm.

"Hi, girls. How were your days?"

"Mr. Mars was mad 'cause I was late to his class," said Maggie, her mouth full.

"Did you give him the note I wrote for you?" asked Charlotte.

"I couldn't find it."

"Josh Porter threw up during lunch," said Sharita. "It was gross."

"Where's Beth?" asked Donna. "I thought we were going to have a special going-away dinner for her tonight. I made her a present."

"I almost forgot," said Maggie. "Mr. Jackson gave me a card to give to Beth. It's in my backpack. I'll go get it. He said all the teachers signed it."

"That's really nice," said Charlotte, feeling deceitful but deciding it best to go along for now. She took a bite of the hot grilled cheese Treasure handed her on a plate.

"Where's Beth?"

"In the bathroom," said Maggie.

"She's always in the bathroom. She has to go all the time," said Sharita. "I think we might be out of toilet paper."

Charlotte's eyes met Treasure's over Sharita's head. How had the girls noticed something she'd missed?

"Isn't she going to eat?" asked Donna.

When dinner was finished, Charlotte breathed a prayer, then called the girls into the living room. They were antsy, hyper tonight. Getting them together was like trying to herd cats. Sharita was in the bathroom now. Donna insisted she couldn't come until she got her present wrapped. Unfortunately no one could remember where they'd last put the tape.

"Quit trying to be Miss Perfect. Just put it in a sack or something," said Maggie.

Which made Donna cry.

Finally they were all downstairs when Maggie remembered her card. She ran upstairs to hunt for it. Donna sat next to Treasure on one of the two ticking-striped sofas. Nikki, holding a tail-thumping Mavis, and Vikki, cradling a less-enthused Jasmine, sprawled on the floor in front of the fireplace. Maggie and Sharita lounged on the other sofa, their heads propped up on its opposite arms.

"Your feet stink," said Sharita.

"Not as bad as yours," said Maggie.

Treasure eased herself into the rocking chair, and Charlotte moved the piano bench over in front of the hearth. She and Beth sat down side by side.

"So you gonna give some kind of a good-bye speech?" asked Maggie.

"I want to give a speech," said Sharita.

"Would you be quiet for one minute?" asked Donna, who had found some tape and was holding in her lap a hastily but neatly wrapped box.

146

Charlotte stepped in. "Beth and I have something we need to talk to you about."

"We already know she's gonna leave tomorrow," said Maggie.

"Actually, she's not," said Charlotte. "Things have changed. Beth isn't leaving Tanglewood after all."

"How come? I thought you was going to that place in Arizona," said Vikki.

"Not Arizona. Colorado," said Nikki.

Visa, one of the white cats, jumped up into Beth's lap.

"So what am I supposed to do with this card?" asked Maggie. "You can give it to her after we've finished talking," said Charlotte. "Right now I want everybody to listen to what I have to tell you."

"What's wrong, Beth?" asked Donna.

Charlotte looked over. Beth had started to cry. She put her arm around her shoulders and pulled her close. Visa jumped down.

"The reason Beth isn't going to Colorado—the reason she's staying here—is that she's going to have a baby."

"She's pregnant?" Sharita slapped her hand over her mouth.

"Who's the father?" said Maggie.

"Is it going to be a boy baby or a girl baby?" asked Nikki.

"Hush now," snapped Treasure. "You girls need to stop running your mouths for one minute and listen to what Charlotte's telling you."

The girls froze.

"This is a really hard time for Beth," said Charlotte. "She only found out this morning. She's scared. She's embarrassed. She's afraid you will be mad at her. What she needs right now is for every one of us to show her how much we love her. I know you have a lot of questions, and I'll try to answer them as best I can. I don't know what will happen when Beth has the baby. She has a lot to think about. What we do know is that she's going to stay here at Tanglewood until the baby comes."

Everyone remained so quiet and still, the only sounds heard in the room were those of Beth sniffling.

It was Donna who finally spoke. She got up from her seat, walked over to Beth, and handed her the gift. "I'm glad you're not leaving. I was going to miss you. This was a going-away present. Now it's just a present. For you." She bent down to hug Beth.

Beth hugged her back.

"It's going to be okay, Beth," said Maggie. "My cousin had a baby. She said it hurt but not all that bad."

"We'll help you take care of the baby when it comes," said Nikki.

"Yeah. We can be the babysitters," said Vikki. "There's enough of us we can have our own club."

Beth blew her nose.

And the doorbell rang.

Before Charlotte could stop her, Nikki jumped up and ran to open the door. Standing on Tanglewood's front porch were eighteen of Ruby Prairie's finest, all of them come to see Beth off.

"Surprise!" yelled Kerilynn.

"We came to wish you bon voyage," said Nomie.

"We came to bring you this cake," said Sassy.

"Came to give you this," said Catfish. "Got you a $50 gift card from Wal-Mart. Thought you might could use it."

"We decided to do this on the spur of the moment," said Kerilynn. "Called Pastor Jock's house, but he didn't answer his phone. Must be out of town." She caught Charlotte's eye. "Honey, it's cold out here on this porch. You care if we come on in?"

"Y'all having a party?" asked Lester once they had crowded in.

"Yes," said Vikki to the group. "We're having a big party, 'cause Beth isn't leaving. She gets to stay here 'cause she's gonna have a baby."

Chapter Fifteen

Tuesday morning reactions at the 'Round the Clock Cafe were mixed. "Crying shame," said Chilly Reed. "Child had everything going for her. Free education. Free room and board. An opportunity to better herself. All down the tube."

"I, for one, would like to take my shotgun to that no-account boy what did this to her," said Catfish. "He better hope I never lay eyes on him again."

"You know who he is?"

"I reckon it was that boy she run off with. He had her up in that cabin a good two weeks."

"That's right, you saw him, didn't you?" said Chilly.

"Night he and Beth took off, that boy was in your store."

Catfish nodded.

Kerilynn appeared at his elbow, coffeepot in hand. "Y'all are talking about Charlotte's Beth, aren't you? Bless her heart. I heard you say boyfriend. What'd he look like?"

"Like a punk kid's all I remember," said Catfish. "Thin build. Brown hair. Needed a haircut. Wore one of them earrings."

Nomie, Ginger, and Alice were seated at an adjacent table.

"Say what you want about the boy." Nomie took a sip of her iced tea. She'd never had a daughter, only three sons. "Takes two to tango."

"It does," agreed Alice. "From what I hear, Charlotte's planning on letting Beth stay on at Tanglewood. I don't know if that's wise. She's got those other little girls to think about."

"What'll they do with the baby when it comes?" asked Ginger.

"Don't know. Maybe she'll put it up for adoption," said Alice.

"Is Beth going to keep going to school?" Nomie wondered.

Chilly answered. "She went today. Saw Charlotte dropping all six of them off at the front door this morning."

"That may not sit well with some of the other mothers," said Alice. "They have their own daughters to consider."

"Don't see what good it would do to keep Beth locked up at home," said Kerilynn. "Last I heard, preg-

150

nancy was not a contagious disease."

"You know what I mean," said Alice. "If you had a daughter who was a good girl, would you want her hanging around a girl who'd gone and got herself in trouble?"

"Beth is a good girl," said Ginger. She wiped a tear. "There's not one of us here who can claim never to have made a mistake. Do you know that child has been in seven different foster homes? Tanglewood makes eight. I for one refuse to sit in judgment."

Alice's eyes softened. "You're right, Ginger. I didn't mean—"

Nomie interrupted. "That little girl's going to have a rough go of it. Can you just imagine what she's going through today? My guess is that everyone in town knows by now."

"Not to mention everyone at school," said Ginger.

"Bless her heart," said Chilly.

"Yes," said Nomie, with meaning. "Bless her little heart."

Pastor Jock began his day on his knees by the side of his bed. "Father, bless my work. Let all I do today be to Your glory. Help me lead this church as You would have me to do. In the name of Your Son I pray. Amen."

He'd been out late the night before, visiting an old seminary friend who lived with his family just outside of Dallas. He and Marc stayed up talking well after Marc's wife and kids had given up and gone on to bed, and it was past one when Jock had pulled into his drive.

As he ate a quick breakfast, he checked the messages on the machine.

"Pastor Jock—" The breezy voice was Kerilynn's. "We've put together an impromptu good-bye party for Charlotte's Beth. Planning to surprise them around seven. Got a cake. Some balloons. Don't know where you are, but if you get this message, hope you can come."

The next one was from Catfish. "Pastor, I just come from Tanglewood. They've got some problems going on over there. Give me a call when you get in."

Ginger's message was difficult to understand. He could tell she was crying. "Pastor, I've got some terrible news. Little Beth isn't going off to school after all. She's—she's—oh, bless her little heart, she's going to have a baby. They need you over there. I hope you get home soon."

News traveled fast.

He got to his office fifteen minutes later than his normal eight o'clock sharp. There were three cars already in the church parking lot.

Three sets of folks, waiting to talk to him about Beth.

Everybody was looking at her. All of her teachers. All of the students. It was bad in American history and algebra, worse in PE. Beth could feel their eyes on her belly. She'd left her backpack at home, opting to carry her books in her arms. Between classes, she held them down low, so as to shield her stomach from view as much as she could.

At lunch, some girls called for her to come sit with them. On another day she would have been grateful for, even flattered by, the invitation, but she shook her head. They'd never asked her to sit with them before.

Her eyes searched the cafeteria until she found Donna, Maggie, and Sharita, who shared the same lunch period. She'd never opened up much to the other Tanglewood girls, but today there was no one else whose company she craved.

When she approached the table, she didn't have to say a word. Maggie moved over, and Donna scooted down to make her a place to sit.

"You okay?" asked Donna. She leaned forward and spoke in a low voice.

Beth nodded. "I'm all right." She concentrated on opening up her carton of chocolate milk.

"Anybody say anything to you?" asked Donna.

"No." No one was saying much of anything. At least to her face. "Some dumb kid in my class asked me if it was true," said Maggie. "I told him it wasn't none of his business."

"I'd tell him to shut up or I'd shut him up," said Sharita. "Nobody's asked me anything. If they did, I'd tell them where they could go."

Beth dropped her head, but smiled. "Thanks. But guys, don't do anything stupid. I don't want to make you get in trouble or anything. This isn't your problem. It's mine."

"But we're sort of sisters. Not really. But in a way. You know what I mean," said Donna. She started to cry. "It makes me mad that people are talking about you."

153

"It makes me mad too," said Maggie.

"Me too," said Sharita.

"I hate knowing that everybody's saying things about me," said Beth. "It's so embarrassing. Especially the guys and stuff."

"You can't really tell," said Donna. She was done crying. "Your stomach's still pretty small."

"It won't be for long," said Maggie. "You should have seen my aunt. She got so big she couldn't paint her own toenails. My grandma had to do it for her."

"I heard one time that when you're pregnant you're supposed to eat for two," said Donna. "You want me to go and get you another tray?"

"No," said Beth. "But thanks. When I went to the doctor she made me watch this video. It said I don't have to eat more. I'm just supposed to eat a balanced diet and drink milk."

"Can you feel it?" asked Sharita.

"What?"

"The baby. Can you feel it?"

"Not really," said Beth. "I feel fat. That's all."

"Does it hurt?" asked Sharita.

"Being pregnant? No. But I've been so tired. You know one time I even fell asleep during Sunday night church. The video said it's normal to sleep a lot."

"Did you know you were pregnant?" asked Sharita.

Beth didn't meet her eyes. "Not really. I mean, not for a long time. But then I got sort of afraid that—well, that something might be wrong. That's when I decided to do the test."

154

"What are you going to do?" asked Donna. "Are you going to keep the baby?"

"I don't know. I don't know anything," said Beth. She took a swig of milk and made a face. "Except that this tastes awful."

Maggie grabbed the carton out of her hand and brought it to her nose. "Pee-yew. This stuff stinks. It's gone bad." She got up to get Beth some more.

"Is Charlotte really going to let you stay at Tanglewood until the baby comes?" asked Donna.

"She says she will. I hope so. If she kicks me out, I don't have any other place to go," said Beth.

"What about your real mom?" asked Sharita.

"She's in Ohio, and she's not doing so good," said Beth. "I haven't seen her since I was in the eighth grade. Kim tried to call her when she found out I was pregnant. I don't know why. I guess it's a rule she has to or something. But my mom can't take care of me. She has issues. Right now she's in some kind of a hospital for people with problems in their heads."

"Like a psychiatric hospital?" asked Sharita. "My cousin had to go into one of those places one time. She hated it. Finally they let her out."

"Even if my mom gets out, I can't stay with her."

"I'm glad you get to stay with us," said Sharita.

"And don't worry. If anybody gives you a hard time, I'll let them have it," said Maggie. "Hurry up. Drink this milk. The bell's gonna ring any second. How much milk you supposed to drink anyway? You want me to bring you one more?"

"You didn't sleep at all last night, did you?" said Treasure. She and Charlotte were folding laundry on the kitchen table.

"Not much." Charlotte rubbed her temples. "I've got a killer headache."

"You've been on the phone all morning. That's enough to give anyone a pain."

"I had to call Ben Jackson at the school. Let him know Beth wasn't leaving after all."

"You have to do anything to get her reenrolled?"

"No. Not since it had only been a few days."

"They going to let her stay in school?"

"For now anyway. Later on, when she gets further along, they won't force it, but he said they'd prefer she'd go homebound. They'll send a teacher out a few times a week to bring her work and pick up what she's done."

"Will she be able to finish her grade?" asked Treasure.

"I don't see why not. She's not due till the middle of July."

"Mr. Jackson give you any trouble?"

"No. He was very nice. Shocked, of course. As we all are. Disappointed. And sorry. He said they've had pregnant girls before, just none lately."

"At least none that anyone knows about," said Treasure. Lots of girls . . ." She trailed off, picked up a towel to fold. "Well, you know. You talk to Kim today?"

"Yes."

"What'd she say about the boy?"

"She's found him."

"No." Treasure dropped the towel. "Really? So fast. Where is he?"

"Pear Springs. Little town an hour south of here. According to school records, he enrolled there back before Christmas. Been going to school ever since."

"And you're sure he's the right one—he's the father of Beth's baby?"

"She says he was the only one."

"Jesus help us," said Treasure. "I know this is not right, but I was hoping Kim wouldn't find him at all. Girl's got enough trouble ahead of her without some knuckleheaded boy sticking his nose in where it don't belong."

"If he's the father, he has a right to know," said Charlotte. "This baby will want to know where it came from. It will need to know. I believe that with every bit of my heart. I also believe Beth hasn't dealt with all of this. They were together for two weeks. Then when she broke her foot, he left her. Alone. I've thought all along that she needed to see him, talk to him face-to-face. When she was in the hospital, I tried to get her to tell me about what happened up in the cabin. She never would."

"I suppose now you know why. You figured out when, exactly, the child got pregnant?" asked Treasure.

"As far along as she is, had to have been while she was at the shelter."

"Bless her heart. Those are not good places for a child

to stay," said Treasure. "I've seen them. No supervision. People all over the place. I just can't get over the fact that she has been pregnant since the day that she came to this house."

"Me either," said Charlotte. "It breaks my heart, and I feel so stupid. I wish I'd known. I wish she would have talked to me."

"You did the best you could," said Treasure.

"I feel like I should have asked more questions, point-blank. I mean, she was alone with that boy for two weeks. I figured—well, you know—but I just didn't want to think about it. At the time, I was barely dealing with everything else that was going on with all the girls. Once her foot healed, I thought Beth was all right."

Treasure looked puzzled. "One thing I can't figure. How in the world did one of them doctors or nurses that took care of her when she broke her foot not know she was pregnant? Didn't they check? Some of that medicine they give her could have been bad for the baby. And what about all those X-rays they did?"

"I asked Kim the same thing. She said they did do a test. And the results were positive."

"What?"

"It was on her chart, but best anyone can tell it just got overlooked. At least that's what the hospital is saying."

"That is not right," said Treasure.

"I know."

"It don't make sense." Treasure shook her head. "The test was there all that time? I read something in the newspaper about a hospital what took out this man's

158

good eye instead of his bad one. Stuff like that is not supposed to happen. They should be more careful."

"What's done is done," said Charlotte. "And would it change anything?"

"I suppose not," Treasure conceded. "So what's Kim going to do about this boy?"

"She's arranging to meet him. Going to tell him about Beth."

"And when is she planning on doing this?"

"Tomorrow. She's bringing him here."

Chapter Sixteen

"Where's Beth?" asked Sharita. The school day was over. She, along with Donna, Maggie, and Vikki, their backpacks, coats, and assorted loose and wrinkled papers in tow, climbed into the back of the Tanglewood van. Nikki, whose week it was to sit in the front, took her place beside Treasure.

"Charlotte picked her up a little early," said Treasure. "Y'all buckle up now." She put the van into gear.

"Why'd she pick her up early?" asked Donna.

Five pairs of suspicious ears waited to hear.

"Now, girls." Treasure looked left, then right, then left again. "If Charlotte picked her up early, that's not necessarily y'all's business. This has to do with Beth, not with any of y'all. There's times it's better to just go along and not be asking so many questions."

Her words, meant to calm, instead set off an anxiety-fueled fray.

159

"Something's wrong, isn't it?" asked Donna. "Something's wrong with Beth."

"She better not be getting sent off someplace," said Maggie. " 'Cause if Beth leaves, I'm not staying either. I'll go with her."

"Me too," said Sharita.

"Did Beth get her baby already?" asked Nikki.

"No, stupid," said Maggie. "She's only four months."

"I didn't know," said Nikki. Her cheeks pinked.

"You girls stop worrying yourselves," said Treasure. It was easy to forget that they, too, had been through a lot the past few days. She spoke over her shoulder to the girls in the back. "Everything's fine, I promise. Beth's not going nowhere. She's not in trouble. And no, Nikki, she didn't get her baby. Honey, it'll be on up in the summer before that baby comes. Here's all it is. Kim's coming this afternoon to talk to Beth. She needed some time to talk with Beth without all of us in the house."

"I need to talk to Kim too," said Sharita.

"Me too," said Maggie.

"Not today, you don't," said Treasure. " 'Cause I've got a nice surprise for y'all."

"I don't want any dumb old surprise." Sharita folded her arms across her chest.

"Fine," said Treasure. "Then you can sit out in the van while the rest of us ride Jasper Jones's horses."

"Horses!" said Vikki. "We get to ride horses?"

"Sure do. I called him up and asked if y'all could come. That's where we're headed right now."

"But what about Beth? She should get to ride too,"

said Nikki. "Some other time, honey." Treasure turned down the road to Jasper's place. "She'll get her chance some other time."

Charlotte had not seen Beth so pale since the afternoon she and Catfish Martin found her at the cabin. But then her foot was broken, and she was in shock. This afternoon, the two of them were sitting at the kitchen table eating an after-school snack of cinnamon toast. Not until Beth had finished her first piece did Charlotte tell her the real reason why she had picked her up early from school.

"Kirby?" Beth whispered. "He's coming here? You said Kim was coming. I thought that was why you picked me up."

"Kim is coming. And she's bringing Kirby."

"But I don't want to see Kirby. I don't want to see him ever again. I thought I wouldn't have to." Beth pushed her plate aside and laid her head facedown on the table. "Please. You don't understand."

Charlotte stroked Beth's hair. "Honey, we have to tell him. He has a right to know. You and he need to talk about what you're going to do after the baby comes. I know that seems like a long time from now, but it's only a few months. Depending on what you decide, there are things we need to take care of."

Beth sat up in her chair and stared at Charlotte with dry eyes. "What do you mean? I'm going to take care of it. It will be my baby. Kim can't have my baby. Kirby sure can't have it. I'm not going to give my baby away."

Charlotte measured her words carefully. "No one is

going to tell you what to do, I promise. But you are going to be sixteen when this baby is born. Sixteen, going into the eleventh grade. Taking care of a baby will be hard. There are other options."

"You mean like foster care? Adoption? No. I won't. I told you, I'm going to take care of my baby myself, and I don't see what Kirby has to do with it. I don't need anything from him. I don't need anything from you or from anybody." Beth covered her mouth with her hand, but not before a deep sob escaped.

Charlotte took Beth into her arms. For a long while she did not speak but rocked her back and forth while the two of them sat side by side. Finally she found the right words.

"There's something you've forgotten, Beth. You and I—we're on the same side here. No one is going to make you do anything you don't want to do. But that doesn't change the fact that if Kirby is the father of this baby, he deserves to be told." A moment passed before she spoke. "Beth, is Kirby the father?"

Muffled. "Yes."

"You're sure."

"I never—until the shelter—I hadn't ever—I mean, I never, except with him."

Charlotte had guessed right. Beth had met Kirby at the shelter prior to coming to Tanglewood. She'd figured that it was there that the two of them had hatched their runaway plan, the one that had led them to the cabin. The cabin where Kirby had abandoned Beth when she got hurt.

162

"When—when are they coming?" Beth still had her head buried in Charlotte's embrace.

Charlotte kissed the top of Beth's head, then drew away to look her in the face. "They'll be here any minute. Go upstairs and wash your face; then come back down."

She looked ready to burst into tears all over again.

"Beth, don't worry. All we have to do is inform him. As the baby's father, he has some legal rights, but he's not obligated to exercise them. From what you've told me, after the way he left you . . . well, I don't expect he's going to want anything to do with your decisions about the baby. After today, he can go on with his life, and you can go on with yours."

Jasper Jones had never seen such a gaggling bunch of females in all of his life. They piled out of the van, talking nonstop. Good thing God had made them all cute, was all he could say. Otherwise a person might not be inclined to deal with any of them.

Treasure had brought along fruit juice and cookies for the girls to eat before they rode. Though he'd never had children, Jasper remembered what it was like to come in from school hungry. Maybe he should offer to get them some cheese and crackers.

"Any of you ever ride a horse before?" he asked the group. Two of them had.

As they finished their snacks, Treasure collected their trash in a sack. Jasper made small talk with the girls, asked them about their school, how they liked Ruby

Prairie. Any minute now they'd be asking to use his bathroom. He didn't mind, just hoped they didn't go and stop up his toilet. From past experiences with his sister's daughters, he knew that girls could be real bad about such as that.

"Girls," said Treasure, when they'd finished up, "listen to Mr. Jones. He's going to give you some instructions, tell you some rules. It's important that you all do just as he says. I don't want anybody to end up hurt. Let's have a good time, but let's all be safe. Understand?"

Jasper appreciated her warnings. One of the things he included in his daily prayers was a request to God to please protect the people who came out to ride. He was careful, but when it came to the horses, they were creatures possessed of minds of their owns. Anything could happen. He just hoped it never did.

Which made it all somehow worse that, in the end, it was not one of the girls, but Jasper Jones himself who ended up hurt.

Charlotte was not prepared to like Kirby Brannon. She dreaded looking him in the eye. Ever since she'd known he was coming to the house, she'd been stacking up grievances like logs on a fire, building her bitter case against him. She listed the facts over and over again in her mind.

If not for Kirby, Beth would not have run away.

She would not have ended up in that cabin.

She would not have broken her foot.

And she would not be pregnant.

So how was it that when she opened the front door of Tanglewood and saw him, looking scared, skinny, and sick with a cold, Charlotte's heart broke?

"Charlotte," said Kim, still out on the porch. "This is Kirby Brannon."

Kirby wasn't the awful, predatory man she'd made him up to be in her mind. He wasn't even a man—just a sad-eyed kid with soft brown curls and ice-cold fingers that trembled when he shook her hand.

It was his touch, that damp handshake, that made it all become plain. Here on her doorstep was a troubled, lonely, sixteen-year-old child who, except for being male, was no different from the ones she sheltered under this very roof. She had to stop herself from scooping him into her arms, telling him everything was somehow, some way, going to be all right.

"Hi, Kirby. I'm Charlotte. Come on in."

She directed him and Kim to settle in the living room while she got them all Cokes. When she returned from the kitchen, Kirby was sitting on the couch beside Kim, slump shouldered, eyes down, looking as though he wished to be anywhere but here.

"Beth's upstairs. I'll go get her," said Charlotte.

She saw Kirby's mouth twitch. He wiped his palms on his thighs.

Please, God, Charlotte prayed as she took the stairs. *Be here. Be with us all. I don't know what to say. I don't know what Beth's going to do. Give her strength. Give him strength. Give Kim and me wisdom. Most of all, give us all grace.*

Charlotte knocked, then opened the door of Beth's room. "He's here."

"I know." Beth was standing at the window. She'd pushed aside the lace curtains and was looking out. "I watched them drive up. He looks the same."

"How was it—seeing him now?"

"Weird. It doesn't really feel like it's been that long since we were at the cabin."

Charlotte touched her arm.

"But it has," Beth finished.

"You ready?" asked Charlotte.

"I guess so," said Beth. "Does—does he know?"

"About the baby? No. Kim hasn't told him. She and I agreed it was best for her not to talk to him about any of this without you present."

"So he doesn't know why he's here?"

"No."

"He's probably mad he had to come."

"He doesn't look mad," said Charlotte. "He looks more scared."

"I'm scared too," said Beth. She stalled. "What's he going to say to me? He's going to think it's my fault he had to come."

"You'll be okay. So will he." *God, please let them be.* She took Beth's hand in her own. "Come on now. You can do this. You're not alone." When Charlotte and Beth got near the bottom of the stairs, Kirby and Kim heard them and turned. When he saw Beth, Kirby stood up but didn't move from his spot.

"Hi, Kirby," said Beth. She didn't meet his eyes.

"Hey," said Kirby. His eyes never moved from her.

Beth took a seat next to Charlotte on the sofa opposite Kirby and Kim. He sat back down, but his gaze stayed fixed upon Beth.

Charlotte hoped Kim would start the conversation, because she didn't know where to begin.

Kirby gave neither of them the chance. Speaking as if he and Beth were alone in the room, he asked, "You doing okay?"

"I'm okay," Beth answered.

"Was your foot broke?"

"Yeah. I had to have surgery."

"Really? Man, I'm sorry. I didn't know. It didn't look that bad."

Charlotte saw color rise in Beth's cheeks. Like a water spigot turned on high, words she'd kept in check for the better part of three months gushed out. "Is that why you left me? Because you didn't think it was broken? How could you do that? I was so scared. If Charlotte and Mr. Martin hadn't found me, what would I have done?" She was crying now. "I couldn't even stand on that foot. How could you just leave me like that?"

Kirby got up from his spot to squat down in front of Beth. Ignoring Charlotte and Kim completely, he spoke. "I came back. That same day. But you were gone. I was so scared. I didn't know what had happened to you. I'm sorry, Beth. I'm so sorry I left." He wiped at his eyes. "All this time, I wondered where you were. They sent me back to the shelter. Every day when new kids came in, I hoped you'd be one of them. Then I went back to live with my uncle. I tried to look you up in a phone book, but I didn't know the lady you stayed with's last name. But I never forgot. I promise, Beth. I never forgot you for a minute. Please. Please. I'm so sorry."

Charlotte's eyes met Kim's. Neither of them spoke. At times in Charlotte's life, she had dismissed the angst of teenagers as only so much drama. But not today. Grief for what yet lay ahead for these two children weighed heavily on her heart.

Kirby took hold of Beth's hand that was now covering her wet face and brought it to his lips. "We can still be together. I'll write you letters every day. Maybe my uncle will let me borrow his truck so I can come see you. Don't you understand? I wasn't going to leave you at the cabin. I just freaked out. But as soon as I got to the road, I knew I was going to get help."

Beth didn't speak. She wouldn't look at Kirby, but she didn't pull her hand away from his grasp.

"What do you want me to say? What do you want me to do?" asked Kirby. "You just tell me, 'cause I'll do anything to show you how much I care about you. Anything. I give you my word."

Beth finally raised her eyes. She shook her head and pulled her hand back.

Charlotte handed them each a tissue. Beth blew her nose. Kirby didn't even seem aware that he had the tissue in his hand. He stayed kneeling in front of Beth, who finally spoke. "You don't have to say anything. You don't have to do anything. That's all in the past."

"You believe me?"

"I guess so." Beth shrank back into the cushions of the sofa. Charlotte could see how fatigued she was.

"Kirby, come sit back over here," said Kim. She patted the spot beside her. "Give Beth a little breathing room."

He did as she said.

"I'm glad you and Beth got to talk about that day at the cabin," said Kim. "I think it was important for you two to straighten things out. But that's not why I brought you here. There's something we need to discuss."

Charlotte felt Beth's body tense.

"There's no easy way to tell you this, so I'm just going to say it right out," said Kim.

Kirby, confused, looked from Beth to Charlotte to Kim and back to Beth. "Is something still wrong with her foot?"

"No," said Charlotte. "Beth's foot is just fine."

"Beth is pregnant, Kirby," said Kim. "She says you are the father."

"You—you're going to have a baby?" His eyes were wide. "When?"

"She's due in July."

For the first time since he'd stepped into the house, Beth looked Kirby square in the eye. His reaction was a test. Charlotte didn't know whether she should hope the boy passed or failed.

"A baby," he said again.

"Beth and I have talked," said Kim. "She doesn't plan

on putting your name on the baby's birth certificate. She doesn't want child support. There's nothing she expects from you, but you had to be told."

"What do you mean? Beth, I love you." He got up to kneel in front of her again. "I'll take care of you. I'll get a job. Two jobs if I have to."

Beth's eyes softened. She let Kirby take her hands.

"Kirby," said Kim, "it's wonderful that you're prepared to take responsibility, but Beth's not asking—"

He cut her off. "Beth, can't we go someplace to talk? Just you and me?"

Kim looked at Charlotte.

"Of course," said Charlotte. "You can go out onto the porch. Kim and I will stay here. Beth, if you need me, just call. Okay?"

Beth and Kirby went outside, and the two women sat in silence for a while. Charlotte fidgeted in her place on the sofa.

"You think she's okay?" asked Kim finally.

"Yes. I do. And I think it's right for them to be able to talk. He's not going to believe Beth wants him out of her life unless she tells him so herself. And believe me, she wants him gone."

"That's really the best thing. Does she know what she's going to do about the baby?"

"She insists that she's going to keep it. I'm still hoping she'll at least consider adoption, but she's so mixed up and emotional right now I'm not pushing."

"She's a strong girl. Stronger than she seems. Amazing, considering the life she's had. There's no

reason she can't go on and make a good life for herself."

Charlotte looked at her watch.

"How long have they been out there?" asked Kim.

"Twenty minutes."

"I still hear them talking."

"I'm surprised they're taking this long."

Kim fiddled with some papers in her satchel. Charlotte picked at the fringe on a throw pillow. Finally the
front door opened up, and Kirby and Beth came back
in.

Hand in hand.

"Kirby, you ready for me to take you home?" asked
Kim, as she and Charlotte rose from their seats.

"Yes," said Kirby, "but first you need to know something." He looked at Beth, who moved to stand closer
to him. "Beth and I have decided what we're going to
do."

"And?" said Kim.

"We're going to get married."

Chapter Seventeen

Jasper could not figure out how it was he'd thrown out
his back. Years of teaching high school ag—hauling
fifty-pound sacks of feed; tugging on the lead ropes of
cantankerous goats, sheep, heifers, and steers; teaching
clumsy students how to build fences—not once had he
ever hurt his back.

Not until now.

If this didn't beat all. Had to happen in front of Treasure. First he'd embarrassed himself near to death throwing up in that helicopter. Now this. Helped to his room by Treasure and her bunch of girls, he eased himself down onto his bed. He wanted to escape when he remembered that on the floor at the end of his bed were yesterday's boxers. From where he lay he couldn't see them, but he knew they were there. Navy blue plaid— right out in the open for all of the world to see.

Could it get any worse?

"Does it hurt here?"

He lay flat while Treasure kneaded and poked. "No."

"How about here?"

"Arrugghhh!"

"Can you feel your toes?"

He could.

"Any numbness? Tingling?"

"No. Don't think so."

He must have wrenched something when he bent down to help Sharita mount her horse. Child wasn't quite tall enough to get her foot into the stirrup to hoist herself up. As he'd done many times before, he bent down and intertwined his fingers, making a place to put her foot. When he felt her weight in his hand, he'd heaved. Sharita went up, but he went down.

"You got any lotion?" asked Treasure.

"Lotion. Why?" He lay facedown on his bed. He wished all these females would go home so he could pick up his boxers.

"I'm going to work on your back. Can't be sure, but I

172

think you've just got a strain. If that's what it is, I can help."

"What are you going to do to him?" asked Maggie.

"You gonna walk on his back?" asked Sharita. "I saw a lady do that on TV."

"No, I'm not going to walk on his back," said Treasure. "I'm going to give him a deep tissue massage—work on his muscles. They're trying to spasm. I'll help them loosen up."

"Where'd you learn to do that?" asked Donna.

"Massage therapy school. Before I came to stay with Charlotte to help take care of y'all, I had my own clinic." Treasure rolled up her sleeves and took off her rings. "You girls sit down now. Right over there."

"You really don't have to," said Jasper. "I think I'm fine. I just need to take some aspirin. I've got a heating pad in one of these closets." He moved to sit up, but a spasm made him groan. Which was worse—the pain in his back, or six pairs of female eyes seeing him like this?

"Shouldn't he go see a doctor?" asked Donna.

"May have to," said Treasure, "but I don't think so. We'll know better after I'm done."

"Really, I'm all right," said Jasper.

"Can we go in the living room and watch TV?" asked Nikki. "Can we go pet the horses?" asked Vikki.

"No. Y'all stay right here in this room," said Treasure. She moved from Jasper's back to his side where she could look him in the eye. "I think I can help you. Maybe save you a doctor visit. But if you don't want me to try, if you're thinking I might make it worse, I won't do a thing. It's up to you."

Jasper didn't want to hurt her feelings. "Oh, no. It's not that I don't trust you. I do. But maybe if I sat up for a minute." He tried but couldn't without awful pain.

Treasure took charge. "That sounds like an okay to me. Pull off your shirt and scoot as close to the edge of this bed as you can get. My clients are usually up on a high table. Low as this bed is, my own back'll be killing me time I get through with you. Maggie—hand me the cushion off that chair. I'm going to start out on my knees. Y'all'll have to help me up when I'm done. Donna, go see if you can find some lotion in Mr. Jones's bathroom."

"Under the sink," he said, knowing he was beat. "Lotion's under the sink."

Charlotte phoned Pastor Jock soon after Kim and Kirby left, to let him know how the afternoon had gone and to request his prayers. "They want to do what?" he asked. Surely he'd misunderstood. "Get married."

"Do they even know each other? They haven't seen each other in almost two months. How old is he anyway?"

"Sixteen. Says he loves her. Maybe he does. I don't know. Beth cried when he left. She's upstairs asleep."

"What are you going to do?"

"I don't know. For sure nobody's getting married. Baby or no baby, that would be a mistake. Both Kim and I thought that the boy wouldn't want to have anything to do with the baby or with Beth. And after the way he left her at the cabin, I didn't think she'd have anything to do with him."

"What changed her mind?"

"He apologized. Told her he had come back for her and she was gone. Said he'd been trying to find out where she was all of this time."

"Right," said Jock.

"You know, I believe he did. The biggest surprise is that he's a likable kid. Not at all what I expected. He's just like Beth. Been tossed around all his life. Lives with his uncle, who's not much older than he is. He says he wants to be around during the pregnancy, and he'll help out with the baby when it comes."

"You think he even knows what that means?"

"I think he doesn't have a clue."

"So where does it go from here?"

"I gave him permission to call. And I told him he could visit as long as I knew when he was coming and he found his own way."

"You're being very generous."

"He's the father of this child. He and Beth have that connection. And you know—no matter what happens, they always will."

Later, as Pastor Jock made evening laps on the cemetery trail, his mind went back to the day when he, like Beth's boyfriend Kirby, had learned he was about to become a dad. He was nineteen, his girlfriend the same. When his girlfriend told him of her pregnancy, his first reaction had been one of sputtering disbelief.

A baby? How had this happened?

To him?

Which of course had to be two of the most universally dumb questions anybody had ever asked in the world.

His second reaction had been one of anger. He didn't want a baby, he'd told his girlfriend. He had plans. Stuff he had to do. What exactly did she expect him to do about it anyway?

She and her parents knew exactly what it was he was to do. Marry her. Support her. Help her take care of the baby.

Which he reluctantly set out to do. Three weeks later they wed in her mother's backyard. His bride wore a too-tight white dress, he black pants, a white shirt, and a borrowed tie. Having been out until two with his buddies the night before, he remembered little about the ceremony other than how queasy and sweaty he'd been as he stood in the sunshine and made his vows.

The marriage didn't last long. Nor did the pregnancy. She had a miscarriage.

And he didn't grieve.

They were divorced within months. No harm done. No hard feelings. That's the way he had looked at it back then. He could go on with his life as though it had never happened. And of course, so could she.

Years passed before he ever grieved the death of his child, his marriage, the pain that his reckless, selfish actions had caused. Was he forgiven?

Yes. He knew he was.

Had he forgotten?

No. Especially not on a day like today.

Jock's steps crunched on leaves as he ran. He faced the western horizon, then glanced at his watch. One more lap and he'd head home. Sunset wasn't far off. In the solitude of the chill February air, his thoughts covered more ground than his feet.

What would that lost baby—his child—have looked like? Would it have been a boy or a girl? If his son or daughter had lived to be born, he or she would be nearly twenty years old today. That thought—and his aching side—made him feel old. And sad.

He prayed as he ran his last lap.

Lord, I'm lonely. You know most of the time I'm okay. But not today. You've redeemed the mess that my life was back then. Given me hope. A purpose. You use me for Your purposes, weak and flawed as I am. I'm grateful. So grateful. All that You've given me should be enough, and most days it is. But not today. Oh, Lord—how I wish I were going home to someone. To a wife. To a child. I had that once. I threw it away. Am I never to have it again?

The last quarter lap, Jock slowed his pace so as to cool down, not saying much else to God. When he got to his truck, he pulled his key from his pocket, put it in the ignition, cranked it, and started to go. Then he shut it back off.

Alone in his truck, Jock leaned his face over the steering wheel and allowed himself five minutes of tears.

Beth heard the door of her room open up. Smelled Charlotte's perfume. She pretended to sleep until she heard the door close and Charlotte's footsteps heading back down the hall. She wasn't ready to go downstairs just yet.

She sat up in bed, hugged her knees to her chest. That wasn't as easy to do as it was when her stomach was flat. She put her hand on the bulge. It seemed like she'd gotten lots bigger in just the past few days. Maybe the baby felt free to grow, now that its little life wasn't a secret anymore.

The doctor had told her she might feel it move pretty soon. What would that be like? Sounded pretty weird. People talked about babies kicking. Would it hurt? Of course having the baby was supposed to hurt. Bad. She'd seen it once on TV. Maybe she'd have to have a C-section. They put you to sleep for that, she'd heard.

Beth got up and went to her desk on the other side of the room. Kirby had given her a picture of himself today just before he left.

"I'll be back," he promised. "I don't know when, but I'm coming back to see you. In the meantime, you look at this picture every day. I'll call you. And I'll write to you. I promise. Don't forget me. Okay?"

She wouldn't forget.

"This is your daddy," she whispered to her baby inside. "When you're ready to be born, you'll get to meet him." She wasn't mad at him anymore. She couldn't be if she tried. Crazy. Even before he'd told

178

her what had happened—before he'd explained about coming back for her, about not knowing how to reach her—she'd felt all mixed up inside. She'd expected to hate him when she saw him. And she had been mad— but at the same time her heart had pounded about a thousand times a minute when she saw him.

She loved him.

No matter what anybody said about fifteen being too young to know—she did know. She and Kirby were meant to be together. Forever.

Wasn't the baby proof of that?

Everyone around the table was talking at once. Treasure's out-of-this-world roast beef, mashed potatoes, salad, and hot rolls were disappearing fast. The smell of cherry cobbler wafted from the oven.

The freezer held vanilla ice cream just waiting to go on top of the rich dessert.

"We didn't get to ride very long," said Maggie, talking with her mouth full.

"I didn't get to ride at all," said Sharita.

"Pass the potatoes, please," said Donna.

"Poor Mr. Jones," said Charlotte after she heard the tale of his injured back. She looked around the table at the faces of these dear ones she loved. It was so good for all of them to be eating a meal together. Even Beth had come down. How long had it been since they'd done something as normal as have a meal together just the eight of them?

She decided right then to strive for normality at

Tanglewood. Beth had five more months to go before her baby came. Life had to go on. For her. And for the other girls. It felt good to be talking about something else, someone else's catastrophe other than Tanglewood's own.

"Is he going to be all right?"

"I think so," said Treasure. She got up to check on the cobbler. "I worked on him. Got him loosened up. He was feeling better by the time we left. Girls and I are going back tomorrow so I can check on him. I'll take my massage table—you know that folding one that's out in the storeroom. Be able to do a better job and not kill my back at the same time."

"Maybe we can ride tomorrow," said Nikki.

"I don't think so," said Treasure. "Jasper doesn't need to be doing any lifting for the next few days."

"I don't want to go if I can't ride," said Maggie.

"Me neither," said Vikki.

"It was boring watching you work on his back," said Sharita. "And it took forever," said Nikki.

"Too bad," said Treasure. "You're ever' one going with me."

"Feeling the need for chaperones?" teased Charlotte.

Treasure didn't answer. Instead she got up to get the ice cream.

Charlotte followed her into the kitchen. "I'm curious. When you had your clinic, did you routinely have a crowd of observers when you were with clients?"

"No."

"Then why are you so set on taking this whole herd

180

with you to Jasper Jones's house?"

"When I had my clinic, I didn't generally take on clients that I had a—well, a personal relationship with."

"I thought so!" Charlotte did not hide her glee.

"Keep your voice down," hissed Treasure. "Last thing I need is those girls goin' on about me and Jasper Jones. Man gets embarrassed easy enough as it is."

"So there is something going on between the two of you," said Charlotte. "And you've lost weight, haven't you? I saw you didn't dish up any dessert for yourself. Now I know why." Charlotte could not stop grinning. "And you're looking really good, I might say. I bet Jasper's noticed. This is wonderful. So, are you—dating, or what?"

Treasure snorted. "You seen me go out on any dates? We aren't doing anything more than just talking. And having coffee. After my riding lessons."

"So it's still a business relationship then," said Charlotte, a bit let down.

"I don't know if I'd exactly call it *business,*" said Treasure. She didn't meet Charlotte's eyes. "He hasn't exactly charged me since, oh—about the second week."

Chapter Eighteen

Lila Peterson pumped on the foot pedal, elevating Kerilynn's chair. "How long has it been since we did these roots?"

"Six weeks. Maybe seven." Kerilynn studied herself in the mirror.

"Six weeks nothing. It's been at least three months." Lila clucked her tongue. She lifted a gray-rooted strand as if it were a snake. "Look at that. You've no business running around like this. As mayor of this town, I'd think you'd take better care of yourself."

"Guilty as charged," said Kerilynn. "I don't know where my time goes. Seems like I'm always on the go."

"Business at the 'Round the Clock good?" Lila leaned Kerilynn's chair back to the sink.

"As always. Thinking of adding a couple new menu items."

"Like what?"

"Maybe a salad plate for the dieters. Seems everybody's trying to cut back." She winced. "That water's a little bit hot."

"Sorry." Lila adjusted the temperature. "Speaking of dieting, have you noticed Treasure Evans? That woman has got to have lost a good twenty pounds."

"Saw her at church last Sunday. She does look good," said Kerilynn.

"They say cutting back on carbs works," said Lila. "I was thinking of trying that. You can eat all the bacon you want. Do you think she's counting carbs?"

"I don't know about carbs," said Kerilynn. "My best guess is that she's counting on something else—like on the attention of that nice Jasper Jones."

"I noticed that," said Lila. She pulled a towel from the cabinet at the side of the sink. "The two of them have been sitting together during Bible study."

"They're in the 'Round the Clock every Friday night for fish."

"Is she a widow?"

"Divorced. Long time ago."

"What about him?"

"Fifty-five years old and never been married."

"Really? He's a handsome man. You know what they say: you're never too old to find your soul mate. No wonder Treasure's losing weight. There's nothing like love to take off the pounds." Lila toweled Kerilynn's hair while she talked. "Speaking of pounds, that little Beth sure is showing. Bless her heart. How far along is she?"

"Believe she's going on five months."

Thumpa-thumpa-thumpa. Dr. Lovington held the wand to Beth's belly.

"You mean that's his heart? Is it supposed to be so fast?" asked Kirby. This was his first doctor visit with Beth. He'd hitchhiked to Ruby Prairie so he could be with her.

"Yes. That's a normal rate. Babies' hearts beat faster than ours do."

"So you're saying our baby is okay," said Kirby.

Charlotte, also in the room, listened but did not interrupt.

Dr. Lovington handed Beth a tissue and helped her sit up. "I think so. Beth's age still puts her at high risk, but we're at twenty-one weeks.

So far everything looks good. Are you taking your vitamins every day?"

"I only missed one," said Beth.

"What about school? Are you still going?"

"Yes. If I want to, they'll let me stay home and send a teacher to me once a week. But right now I'm going every day."

"Good. As long as you feel well and are getting enough rest, I think it's best that you keep going to school. You need to get out. Pregnancy is not the same as being sick. And be sure you're getting some exercise every day. Doesn't have to be anything really strenuous. A thirty-minute walk would be good."

Beth nodded.

"Any questions?" Dr. Lovington made notes in Beth's chart. "All right, then. How about we see you in three weeks? Suzie will make you an appointment on your way out."

Over slices of Italian cream cake and cups of hot tea, the ladies of the Ruby Prairie Culture Club, minus Charlotte, who was home with a sinus infection, were engaged in a touchy debate.

"Now, I'm not judging," said Nomie, "but there was a time when girls like that went away to some home."

"They may have gone away, but everybody knew where it was they had gone," said Alice. "I for one don't see what good it does anyone to treat an unwed mother like she's some kind of a second-class citizen."

Kerilynn tried to soothe the tension. "No one's talking about second-class anything. The question is whether or not the club gives Beth a baby shower."

"We give one for every other girl who's got a close relative in the club," said Sassy.

"But if we give Beth onc, what message does that give to the girls who are behaving themselves?" asked Nomie. "Wouldn't that be saying that the trouble Beth has gone and got herself into is just fine and dandy?"

"I do see Nomie's side," said Alice. "It doesn't seem right to honor a girl who—well, who you know."

Kerilynn tried to speak, but Alice held up her hand.

"I know. You don't have to tell me. We should help out. Land knows, Charlotte's going to need every bit of help she can get, and we all love Charlotte. That's not the question. We love those girls, too, Beth included. I think we prove that every week. There's not a one of us who doesn't support Tanglewood in some way. But I'm not comfortable giving a party for a girl who hasn't done the right thing. It will be awkward. For her. For us. For everyone, as I see it."

"That doesn't change the fact that there's a baby coming, one that will need lots of things," argued Ginger.

Kerilynn spoke up. "I think we're in agreement that we want to help out. How about a money tree? We could give it to her in private. Spend the same amount we all would if we were buying gifts."

"Why go to the trouble of a money tree?" said Alice. "Let's just get her a gift card from Wal-Mart. She and Charlotte can go down there and get whatever they need."

Several club members murmured their agreement.

But not Lucky Jamison. Aided by her cane, she rose to her feet.

Kerilynn motioned for everyone to give Lucky the floor. Bless the poor woman's heart; she wasn't in good health. They should have been more careful about discussing such a sensitive topic in her presence.

"I apologize, Miss Jamison, for such frank talk," said Nomie, red faced.

"I do too," said Alice. "That is a lovely dress you have on. It must be new."

Lucky didn't acknowledge either comment. "Times have changed," she began. "For the better. Of course a girl should have a ring on her finger before she has a child. That's God's way. But people make mistakes. I certainly have. An innocent child is about to be born. A baby. A gift from heaven. That Beth is a precious girl. She and the others have been coming to my home once a week for the past three months. I'm teaching them how to cook, how to sew, how to keep house. Beth is a smart girl. She has good manners. I've grown fond of her. I'll have no part of slipping her some kind of a discount store card like we were ashamed to even know her. If none of you are inclined to host a shower for her, I'll do it myself."

Alice coughed.

Nomie cleared her throat.

No one in the room met Lucky's eyes.

Finally Kerilynn called for a vote.

It was unanimous. Beth's shower was set for April the nineteenth.

Kirby and Beth sat shoulder to shoulder in a wicker swing on Tanglewood's front porch. The warmer March weather made it pleasant for them to be outside, which was good, because outside was the only place they could talk. Charlotte was pretty nice, Treasure too, but all of those girls got on his nerves.

"What do you think it'll be? A boy or a girl?" he asked.

"I think it's a girl," said Beth.

He thought a boy. "Can't they do some kind of test to find out?"

"They did. A sonogram. Two of them. But the baby wasn't turned right. They couldn't see."

"Can you feel it move?" asked Kirby. He'd seen on TV that you could.

"Sometimes," said Beth. She put his hand on her belly. He held it there for a long time.

"I don't feel anything."

"I guess she's asleep," said Beth. "No, there it goes. Did you feel that?"

He pretended that he did. They sat in silence for a long moment. He'd written more than ten letters. Beth had written back twice. Sometimes his uncle let him call. He'd come to Tanglewood three times in the past five weeks. Finding a ride to Ruby Prairie wasn't easy. Some guy doing work over here was giving him a ride home today. Each time he came it was weird at first. Like he and Beth didn't know for sure what to say to each other.

"It was cool hearing the heartbeat," he finally said.

"Hard to believe there's a really little person in there."

"I'm getting fat," said Beth. "I can't wear any of my jeans anymore."

"You're not fat. I mean, not anywhere but your stomach."

Kirby held Beth's hand and played with the silver ring she wore on her thumb. They hadn't even kissed since that last time at the cabin. He wanted to. He wondered if she did too.

"I wish I didn't have to go back to my uncle's. I hate it there," said Kirby. "You're here and I'm not. I think about you all the time. Kids at school, they ask me what's up. I can't tell them. They'd just say stuff if they knew. Sometimes I don't feel like talking to nobody. I'm just thinking about you. And about the baby."

Beth didn't speak, but she didn't pull her hand away.

"I've been working with my uncle after school and on the weekends. Doing construction." Actually his uncle did construction. They let him clean up. "Look. I got paid." He dug in his pants pocket, pulled out two twenties. "This is for you. For the baby."

You don't have to give me money," said Beth.

"Yes, I do." Why did she say that? He wanted to do his part. "I want to. Maybe you can get yourself some of those pregnant pants. Pretty soon I'll have a lot more."

Beth held the bills in her hand. "What's going to happen to us?" she finally whispered.

"What do you mean?"

"I never expected to see you again. Not after the

188

cabin. But then I did. When Kim brought you here and told you about the baby, I didn't think I'd see you after that. But now—you're back again. You keep coming back. I don't know what to think."

"You don't trust me, do you?" Kirby asked.

"I want to. But I'm afraid. What if this time, or the next time, or the one after that, you decide you don't care about me anymore?"

"That's not going to happen," he said. "When we were at the cabin, even before that, when we were at the shelter, you said that you loved me. Do you still?"

"Yes, but—"

"We love each other. That's all that matters. I'll come back every time I can. I'll be here for you. You may not believe it now, but I'll prove it. Just give me a chance. We're going to be together forever, Beth. We have to be. If we love each other, they can't keep us apart. They say we can't get married right now, but when the baby comes, maybe Charlotte will let me stay here."

"I don't know," said Beth. "She only takes girls."

"Then I'll get an apartment or something. I can go to school here. Get a job. Whatever it takes. When we're eighteen we'll get married. They won't be able to stop us then."

Beth wasn't saying much. She never did.

"Promise me, Beth. No matter what happens, don't give up on us. I'm scared of losing you. If we broke up I don't know what I'd do." He wiped at his eyes with the back of his sleeve.

He hated that he was crying, but he couldn't help it.

Never before in his life had he been as sure of anything as he was of how much he loved Beth.

Please.

She had to love him back.

Because no one else in the world did.

Chapter Nineteen

"You need some antibiotics," said Treasure. "You've been sick with your sinuses going on a week. If you were going to get better on your own you would already have done it by now."

Charlotte sipped a cup of peppermint tea. "I'm better. Really. I don't have any fever, and my headache is less than it was yesterday."

Treasure passed Charlotte one of the lemon bars Ginger Collins had brought over. "Take care of yourself is all I'm saying. Won't be any good to anybody else if you don't look after your own health first."

"Speaking of health—how's Jasper's back?"

"Doing good. Thanks to his taking it easy and my giving him a massage twice a week."

"How much longer will he be needing those?"

Every time Treasure went to Jasper's, she made all six girls come along, despite their whining and complaining. Evidently she felt the need to be chaperoned.

"Probably not more than another session or two. Maybe three."

"You've really helped him. Do you miss your business?"

They'd never talked about how long, exactly, Treasure planned to stay at Tanglewood. What a godsend she had been. Those first few months in Ruby Prairie—it had been one crisis after another getting the home up and running. Friends and neighbors had helped out, once Charlotte gave in and let them, but it was the day-to-day presence of Treasure that was such a blessing.

"Actually, I hadn't missed it much until Jasper got hurt," said Treasure. "You know I'd been having such trouble with carpal tunnel that if I hadn't taken a long rest, I likely would have had to quit. But yes, I do miss it. I've even been thinking about renting a little place here in Ruby Prairie that I could work out of. You think it would go over?"

Charlotte tried to hide her delight. "Yes. I mean I suppose some folks might be a little suspicious at first."

"Probably think I was some kind of a pervert." Treasure laughed.

"But soon as word got around that you're able to help people feel better, I think you'd have more work than you'd know what to do with." Charlotte paused to sip tea. "So. Does this mean what I hope it means? Are you planning on staying in Ruby Prairie? Staying here at Tanglewood?"

"I've been giving it some thought. I've put it to prayer."

"Does Jasper Jones have anything to do with those thoughts and prayers?"

Treasure feigned innocence. "He's a good friend. A good riding teacher."

"And a good person to eat fish with on Friday nights," teased Charlotte.

"We're two middle-aged folks what enjoy each other's company, that's all."

"I'd like nothing better than for you to stay here forever," said Charlotte. "I don't know what I'd do without you."

"You've got your feet under you now. What with the ladies coming to help out on a regular basis and the menfolk from the church taking care of the yard and van, I think that if I did leave, you'd do fine on your own."

"But I thought you were thinking of staying."

"I don't have any plans to leave," said Treasure, "but if I do open up a clinic, it would take me away from this house some of the time. And someday I might decide I want to get me a little place of my own."

"Well, of course. I didn't expect you to live here forever." Although she had hoped that Treasure would.

"Honey, as attached as I am to you and these girls, I'm always going to be close by," said Treasure. "With this baby coming on, I know you'll be needing extra help. I'm not planning on going anywhere until well after that."

Charlotte breathed out relief. "Good. I never want you to feel obligated, but I don't know anything about babies. I've been counting on you to teach Beth and me everything we need to know."

"So it's settled? Beth's going to stay on at Tanglewood?" asked Treasure. "With her baby?"

"That's what she wants. I don't know where else she would go."

"What about that boy? I figured he'd be long gone by now, but seems every time I turn around he's either calling or knocking on the door."

"I know it. I thought the same thing. He's only sixteen, but he's sure devoted to Beth and this baby. You should have seen him at the doctor's appointment. Couldn't take his eyes off the sonogram screen. Asked the doctor a million questions."

"What about Beth? You think she feels the same way about him?"

"She loves him. I know she does. Remember—that first time he came she was ready to marry him."

"Crazy kids," said Treasure.

"I also think she's afraid to trust him. Afraid he's not really going to stick around."

"Sixteen-year-old boy? Still wouldn't surprise me none if he took off and we never saw hide nor hair of him again," said Treasure.

"You may be right. All I know is that these two kids have made a baby," said Charlotte. "It's done. And forever, they will be the parents of this child, whether they stay together or they break up. I'm certainly not encouraging them to get married, but I am encouraging Kirby to be involved."

"Bless their hearts. They need all the prayers and the hope they can get."

Treasure left to get her hair fixed. No one in Ruby

Prairie did African-American hair, but there was a woman in Ella Louise who worked out of her house.

"She's slow, but she knows what she's doing," Treasure said before she left. "May be after supper before I get back."

When the girls were home, Tanglewood was a noisy, active place. During the day, Charlotte and Treasure worked companionably side by side, assisted by the helpful Ruby Prairie ladies. Despite the gratitude she felt for their invaluable help, Charlotte enjoyed the occasional rare hours she had alone.

Soon as Treasure had gone, she put a load of clothes into the dryer, started another load washing, and took out two pounds of ground beef to thaw for supper. She mopped the kitchen and dusted the living room. Finally she granted herself a seat in the swing on Tanglewood's wraparound porch and began to push herself back and forth with her toe.

Snowball hopped up onto her lap and settled in for a nap, undisturbed by the metallic squeak of the swing. Charlotte stroked the white cat. She blew her nose. Talk of babies had rubbed raw a tender spot in her heart. Most of the time she kept close rein on her thoughts, but in this quiet moment she let them fly free. So much had happened in such short a time. It was only March. She'd opened Tanglewood's doors to her girls in September. While months of prayer and planning had gone into its opening, she never dreamed that before it celebrated its first year as a girls' home, the pink-and-white house would be home to a newborn baby.

Next month was Beth's shower. Soon they'd need to begin fixing a nursery in the corner of Beth's room, stocking up on diapers and wipes. She should look into childbirth classes. Would Kirby want to go? Probably, if he could find transportation. It was difficult to believe Beth was more than halfway through her pregnancy.

Charlotte and J.D. had never gotten this far. There had been years of trying to have a baby, the ecstasy of finally getting pregnant, followed by the devastation of a miscarriage. Seeing Beth get bigger and bigger brought it all back.

J.D. had teased her about wearing maternity clothes so early. He was right; she hadn't needed them. But after gazing enviously at the swollen bellies of friends and family for so many years, she couldn't wait. *But my regular clothes are getting too tight,* she'd explained. Never mind that she was only six weeks along. She remembered a particularly corny T-shirt loaned to her by a friend. *Baby,* it said, with a huge arrow directed to her middle.

She wanted everyone to know.

Which made it all the harder when, at nine weeks, she began to bleed.

She'd done nothing wrong, her doctor had explained. Best thing to do? Wait a couple of months and try again. He patted her hand. Now that she'd been pregnant once, she'd likely find herself that way again really soon.

She never did.

After a few years they gradually quit talking about it.

They no longer scheduled romance for particular times of the month.

When had she given up hope? Had she ever? The month before J.D. died, at age thirty-nine she'd found herself five days late. Not wanting to disappoint him, she'd not told him. Which had turned out just as well, since it was a false alarm.

Boots Buck drove past the front of her house. He honked and waved. Charlotte waved back. Boots and Alice had never had children either. How was it that devoted, happily married, careful-of-every-detail-of-their-health couples sometimes couldn't have children, while unmarried teenagers who kept crazy hours and ate mostly chips and sodas made babies in the backseats of cars without giving it any thought?

It wasn't jealousy she felt toward Beth, but something uncomfortably akin. *God forgive me. Help me. You know how much I wanted a baby. You've given one to Beth. Help me to love it, to care for it as long as You let me be a part of its life.*

That was the hard part. Not knowing what lay ahead. The thought of having a baby to care for, even if it wasn't her own, was delicious. She couldn't wait to hold it, to smell it, to feel its little soft head up under her chin. *Better watch yourself,* Nomie Jenkins had warned. You'll *get attached to that baby when it comes.*

How, exactly, was one supposed to *not* get attached?

And how would Beth behave when the baby came? Would she, a child herself, hand the baby over to her and Treasure, or would she be possessive and want to do everything for it herself? Which would be better? For her? For the baby? And what about when Beth went back to school? Charlotte was only learning how to parent teens. How did one parent a parent?

Beth would be sixteen when the baby came. She and Kirby were still talking of marriage—granted, he more enthusiastically than she, but what if when the child was two, they did get married? What if they moved away? How would she bear it?

When she first opened Tanglewood, people warned her not to get too attached. Girls would come and girls would go. And though she still had her original six, Charlotte knew that would change. Nikki and Vikki, living at Tanglewood while their mother was treated for cancer, would likely leave in early June. Donna's dad's job—the one that had left his daughter with nowhere to stay—was playing out. He could come back home any-time, and when he did there was nothing to stop him from coming to Tanglewood and picking her up. Donna lived for the day she could go back and live with him.

Charlotte had known it would be that way all along. Yet, despite the warnings of well-intentioned if unin-formed folks, she'd allowed herself to fall impossibly in love with every one of them. How could she not? Early on, she'd vowed to treat every girl who arrived as if she were going to be at Tanglewood the rest of her life.

"It's going to break your heart when your first girl leaves," Treasure had said to her one day.

"If it does," Charlotte answered, "then I'll know I've done it right."

Chapter Twenty

Charlotte took a seat in the reception area and glanced at her watch. For once, she was actually on time—no, not just on time, but five minutes early for the girls' quarterly progress meeting. She smoothed her skirt down over her knees. No matter how many of these sessions she attended, something about being summoned to the principal's office, even if it was by Ben Jackson, always made her palms sweat and her stomach churn.

Perhaps it was not ever knowing what to expect. At the girls' last meeting, she'd gone in confident. According to their report cards, the girls were all making passing grades. She and Treasure had made an extra effort to be vigilant about math homework and spelling words. Any reasonable parent would have seen little cause for concern.

Right?

That was the meeting where she'd learned that Maggie and Sharita had brought lizards to school in punctured sandwich bags. At lunch the poor creatures had gotten loose. When some boys caught them and cut their tails off with art scissors, claiming that the animals would grow new ones, Maggie and Sharita had pelted them with handfuls of mashed potatoes and peas.

Charlotte was still in awe. How was it that not one of the girls had told her about the incident? Nikki and Vikki generally kept her informed. So bad—or good, depending how you looked at it—were they about tattling on the others, Charlotte vacillated between correcting them for carrying tales and pumping them for useful information about the other four. Maggie and Sharita must have either bribed or threatened the two to keep quiet.

"Charlotte. Good to see you. Come on in." Ben motioned Charlotte into his office. "Mrs. Howe, the school counselor, will be joining us, along with a couple of teachers from the middle school hall and two from the high school. They should be here in about ten minutes. Give us a chance to catch up. How've you been?"

"Good. Really good," said Charlotte. Ten minutes? Had she come at the wrong time?

"Missed you at church Sunday. Were you there?"

"No. I was a bit under the weather. Sinus infection. I'm better now."

"Wonderful. This is a bad time for allergies for everyone. We've lots of kids with stopped-up heads and itchy eyes. Keeping Nurse Medford busy."

Ben ran his fingers through his black hair and took a seat behind his desk. When Charlotte was in school, all her principals had been really old. Looking back, probably not more than forty, but still—they'd all had a good ten years on Ben Jackson. How did someone get such a position at such a young age? But according to other parents, and from her limited experience, he appeared to do a good job. He was blessed with compassion, a good sense of humor, and uncanny wisdom when it came to dealing with kids.

199

"Are you nervous?" he asked.

Charlotte realized she'd been chewing on a nail.

"Should I be?"

"No. Not today. Not as far as I know."

"No more leaping lizard incidents?" asked Charlotte.

"Well—no lizards, but there was that problem last week with the snake—"

Charlotte's mouth dropped open.

"Just kidding!" Ben laughed. "No. Everything's been fine. I don't think there'll be any major surprises this afternoon."

And there weren't. At least until after the meeting was over. That was when Ben walked Charlotte all the way out of his office, down the long school hallway, and out to her van. "Remember back a few weeks, when we were working to get Beth's records together so she could leave for Wings of Gold?"

"You were really helpful. I so appreciate it," said Charlotte. "With everything that's happened since then, that seems like a long time ago."

"More than a month," said Ben. "You've probably forgotten something I asked you back then."

No, she hadn't. Charlotte turned bright pink.

"I asked if you'd like to go out to dinner."

"Yes. I remember. You did." Her heart pounded, and she struggled to meet his blue eyes. Not in more than twenty years had she been asked out on a date. That was what was happening—wasn't it?

"At the time, I told you we'd wait until things settled down for you." Ben smiled. "But forget that. If we're ever going to share a meal, it will have to be between Tanglewood crises."

"There is always something going on," Charlotte agreed. She was busy. Really busy. Couldn't he see?

"So. How about Friday night? Joe Fazoli's cousin is visiting from New York. Guy plays acoustical guitar, so Joe's getting him to perform at the restaurant this weekend. It's not often you get dinner with live music right here in Ruby Prairie—unless, of course, you count the Hardy brothers quartet when they set themselves up next to the hot dog stand at the Culture Fest."

While Ben had been issuing his invitation, Charlotte had been digging in her purse for her keys.

"So—would you like to go?"

How did one handle a situation like this? "Um, sure. I like guitar music. And I like Joe's. You want me to, uh, meet you there?"

"I thought I could pick you up," said Ben.

This was definitely a date. "Okay. Sure then. That would be fine."

"Seven?"

"Great."

"See you then."

Cloudy all day, suddenly rain began to fall.

"Better go," said Ben. He turned and sprinted back toward the school.

Charlotte finally she found her keys, unlocked the van, and climbed in. What had she gotten herself into? Ben Jackson was ten years younger than she was.

Friday night at Joe's. Place would be packed. Ruby

Prairie matchmakers would have them married by Sunday. And what was she supposed to tell the girls? Not to mention Treasure?

He was nice enough, a good principal and a supporter of Tanglewood girls. But she wasn't interested in him. Not like that. Why had she said yes? How did a woman turn down a man for a date? She didn't know. It had been too long.

Charlotte started the van and put it in gear. It began to rain harder. Unable to see, she reached for the windshield wiper knob, missed it, and accidentally turned on her emergency flashers instead.

Jasper Jones's back was much improved.

"You were so helpful to me," he said over Friday night catfish at the 'Round the Clock. "It doesn't feel right, you giving me all those massages for free. Why don't you let me pay you?"

"No. Not going to do it," said Treasure. She, forgoing Kerilynn's homemade tartar sauce, squeezed lemon on her fish. "If it wasn't for you giving free riding lessons to the girls, you wouldn't have gotten hurt in the first place. Let's say we're even."

She was like that. Generous to a fault. "Still believe I've come out on the best end of the stick," said Jasper.

"You say that now," Treasure teased. "But you'd be singing a different tune if your back wasn't all right."

"When you coming out to ride?" asked Jasper. He hadn't been on a horse in two weeks. Nor had Treasure been out to his house without hauling all six girls with her. He wasn't sure which he missed the most.

Treasure had never said anything, but he'd under-stood why she brought all those girls along. Chaper-ones. Riding horses and having coffee at his kitchen table was one thing. Giving him massages in his bed-room was another thing entirely.

"How about next week, if your back's still doing good?"

"Monday?" He hoped she'd say yes.

"I may have forgotten everything you showed me, been so long since I rode."

"It'll all come back. Like riding a bike," said Jasper.

Kerilynn refilled their iced teas.

"Can you hand me another packet of Equal?" asked Treasure. "My fish are thirsty."

"Did you have a good time?"

Ginger Collins had come over to stay with the girls while Charlotte and Treasure were out. Charlotte chose her because she was the woman least prone to gossip in the entire town. "It was very nice."

"I didn't think you'd be back so early."

"I'm pretty tired." Charlotte yawned. She'd told Ben the same thing. Had they had a good time? Sure. Sort of. She guessed.

It was after lasagna but before ice cream cones that she'd made it plain to him that she really only wanted a friend. Though she'd gotten vibes that wasn't what he'd hoped for, Ben had graciously covered well. He saw no reason why they couldn't enjoy dinner together every once in a while.

"The music was wonderful. Joe's cousin is really talented."

"Lester and I are going tomorrow," said Ginger. "I love those meatballs Joe makes. Has he put in his ice cream machine yet?"

"Sure has. Chocolate, vanilla, and swirl. Everybody all right here?"

"They're fine. I made them popcorn. Burned the first batch. Your microwave's got more power than mine. I set off the smoke detector. Can you smell it?"

"Only a little bit. Be gone by morning." Charlotte gave Ginger a hug. "Thanks so much for coming. Were there any calls?"

"Just one," said Ginger. "Pastor Jock. I told him I was babysitting while the two ladies of the house were out on dates."

Charlotte's stomach lurched. "It wasn't exactly a date—"

Ginger didn't acknowledge her words. "He said he hoped you were both having a good time, and he'll call back later."

"Any idea what he wanted?"

"He didn't say. Probably something to do with the church."

In his dark living room, Jock channel surfed. Fifty-six channels, and nothing was on.

Out on a date? With whom? He'd never thought Charlotte would be so inclined. Hadn't her husband died just a few months ago? He counted back. No. It had been more like a year. Well, good. He was happy for her. She deserved a little time for herself. Of course she did.

He turned off the TV, picked up Max Lucado's newest book, read three pages, and put it down. He had called to see if Charlotte had any extra buckets that the Lighted Way youth could use for tomorrow afternoon's car wash, as well as to see how many of her girls planned on volunteering their time. He reached for the nail clippers he kept next to his chair. Where had she gone on her date? Out to eat? To a movie? The closest one was a good forty-five minutes away.

From down the hall, Jock thought he heard the toilet running. He got up to check. No. Must have imagined it. Everything looked fine. He sat back down, finished clipping his nails, tried to read again, then decided he needed a snack.

But he was out of graham crackers.

Which meant he had no choice but to make a trip to the store. Could he help it if, in order to get there, he had to drive right past Tanglewood?

Charlotte's van and Treasure's vehicle were both in the driveway. Looked like every light in the house was turned on. Through the lace curtains, he thought he saw Charlotte. So. Not yet ten o'clock, and she was already home. Rather than call her again, he might as well stop. Ask her about those buckets, pick them up if she had any.

Jock's knuckles hadn't even made contact with the

front door before Charlotte, pale-faced and wide-eyed, flung it open.

"Oh, Pastor, I thought you were the ambulance," she said.

"Ambulance? What's happened?"

"It's Beth. Something's wrong. I think she's in labor. And it's way too soon."

Chapter Twenty-one

Ruby Prairie's volunteer ambulance crew, siren blaring and lights flashing, pulled up right behind Jock. "What's happened?" Gabe Eden, chief of the volunteer fire department and head paramedic on the rescue squad, was the first one inside.

"It's Beth," said Treasure.

"The one having the baby?"

"Yes. She's barely six months, but I think she's in labor. Maybe she's not. I don't know."

"Where is she?" asked Gabe.

"Upstairs in her room. Charlotte's with her."

Gabe motioned for one of his crew to bring in a stretcher. "What's wrong?" asked Nikki.

"Why's the ambulance here?" asked Donna.

All five girls, the movie they'd been watching forgotten, stood blinking in the brightly lit entry. The front door stood open. Outside, emergency lights cut through the darkness.

Jock took charge. "It's Beth. She's not feeling well. The ambulance is going to take her to the hospital. Let's go into the kitchen, okay? We need to get out of the men's way so they can get her."

Not one of the girls moved.

Gabe and another member of the crew, with Treasure bringing up the rear, squeezed past to head up the stairs.

Sharita and Maggie started to follow.

"Wait, girls. You can't go up there," said Jock.

"Why not?" They whirled around.

"I want to go up," said Donna.

"I need to get something out of my room," said Maggie.

"Me too," said Nikki.

"I'm sorry, but no one's going up there," said Jock. "I know you want to see what's happening, but we need to stay down here out of the way so they can see after Beth."

"Is something wrong with her baby?" asked Maggie. "One time my cousin—"

Jock cut her off. "We don't know what's wrong. That's why the ambulance is here. My guess is that they'll take her to the hospital where they can do whatever needs to be done for her and her baby. In the meantime, let's move out of the way."

Donna started to cry. So did Nikki and Vikki. Reluctantly they allowed Jock to ease them all into the kitchen, where they sat down around the table.

"Come on, everybody. Sit down. Let's get you all something to drink. Who wants juice?"

Before he could get to the refrigerator, the phone rang. Jock answered it.

Catfish had been listening to his scanner. What was

going on? Jock started to tell him, but Catfish cut him off. Never mind. He and Kerilynn would be right over.

Lester and Ginger let themselves in the back door. Their house was located only half a block from Tanglewood, so they'd seen the ambulance lights from their bedroom window.

"What's happened?" asked Lester, still in his house shoes. "Somebody hurt?" asked Ginger.

Jock filled them in.

"Bless her heart," said Ginger. "She didn't say a word to me when I was here looking after the girls earlier. Do they think she's losing the baby? Isn't it way too soon?"

Jock's eyes cut to the girls, sitting around the table, their ears keened to hear every word.

Lester cleared his throat.

Ginger caught her gaffe.

"We really don't know anything," said Jock. "And I don't think we will until she gets to the hospital and the doctors check her out."

"Where're they taking her?"

"On to Dallas, is my guess. That's where her doctor is."

"Bless her heart," said Ginger again.

"Pastor," said Lester, "I believe we need to have prayer." Just then Nomie and Sassy knocked on the back door.

"We just heard," said Nomie. The two of them bustled in, arms laden with foil-wrapped, nine-by-thirteen-inch pans. "Got a coconut sheet cake in this pan. Sassy's got a berry cobbler in that one."

The ladies set them on the counter.

"Lester, there's paper plates and cups in my backseat. You mind getting them? How's she doing? Anybody started the coffee?"

Jock was not surprised by Nomie and Sassy's quick culinary response to the crisis at Tanglewood. Over and over he'd seen the women of Ruby Prairie respond like this. No matter what the situation, a bunch of them would arrive carting containers of well-prepared food. How did they manage to show up so fast? He didn't know. What he did know was that these were only the first of many more helpful folks who would show up tonight to lend whatever aid they could.

Sure enough. Through the window over the kitchen sink, he saw the headlights of two more cars pulling in.

Treasure stuck her head into the kitchen to check on the girls. "How's Beth?" Jock voiced the question everyone wanted to know.

"Don't really know anything yet. She may be in labor. They're coming down the stairs with her now."

"Can we see her?" asked Donna.

"We want to tell her bye," said Maggie.

"Tell you what," said Treasure. "Y'all go out this kitchen door. Stay off the sidewalk so they can get through. You can say good-bye, but quick. They're in a hurry to get her to the hospital."

The girls all shot out the back door. Not until they were gone did Treasure notice Lester and Ginger, Nomie and Sassy. She hugged them. "Sweet of y'all to come. I know it'll mean a lot to Charlotte."

"What can we do?" asked Nomie.

"How is Beth?" asked Ginger.

"I'm afraid she's probably in labor." Treasure shook her head. "Can't they give her medicine to stop it?" asked Sassy.

"That's what she needs. 'Course Gabe and his crew don't carry anything like that on their truck. That's why they're going to do their best to get her to the hospital."

"Are you going with Charlotte?" asked Jock.

"I feel like I should, but somebody's got to be here with these girls."

"You go on," said Lester. "Ginger and I'll stay."

"Yes," said Nomie. "Go on. Charlotte shouldn't be alone. Don't worry about a thing. We can look after the girls."

Treasure went to the hall closet and got Charlotte's purse and her own. Charlotte would ride in the ambulance. She would follow in her van. She came back into the kitchen.

"Oh, dear," she said. "I don't have any cash. Charlotte doesn't either. I heard her say this morning she needed to go to the bank."

"You'll need some for parking," said Nomie. She reached into her bag.

"And you'll both need food money." Sassy plucked a twenty and a ten from her bosom.

"May need to get a hotel," said Lester. He and Jock both emptied their wallets.

By the time she headed out the door, Treasure had more than a hundred dollars in her purse. "Thank you. Thank you so much. Y'all keep up with how much you gave, and soon as we're back we'll repay you."

They went out the back door just in time to see Gabe helping to load Beth into the ambulance. Charlotte stood to the side while they secured the stretcher and got things inside set up for the transfer.

A growing crowd gathered round to offer words of hope. "Y'all be careful."

"We'll be praying."

"Could be false labor."

"Don't worry about anything here."

"We love you."

From inside the ambulance, Gabe motioned for Charlotte to get in.

Jock managed a last word with Charlotte. Taking her damp hands in his own, he said, "I'm so sorry this is happening. We will pray. Besides that, is there anything you need me to do? Anything at all?"

She hesitated for only a second. "Yes. There is. Try to find Kirby. His uncle's number's on the corkboard over the hall phone. If you find him, bring him to the hospital. Beth's asking for him." She wiped at unbidden tears. "And he should be here."

"Consider it done," said Jock. "I'll find him. Tell Beth that I give her my word."

"Ready?" Beth heard the ambulance driver asking from somewhere up front. She lay on a stretcher on one side of the ambulance. Charlotte sat across from her on a long narrow bench, holding tightly to her hand.

Gabe, near her head, answered, "Let's go."

"Lights and siren?" the voice from up front asked.

When she saw Gabe nod, Beth squeezed Charlotte's hand even tighter.

"You're going to be fine," Charlotte said.

"May be a little bit bumpy at first, but once we're on the interstate, the ride will smooth out," said Gabe. "I'm going to leave this blood pressure cuff on your arm. It won't hurt. Need you to keep the other arm straight for me, okay? I'll be starting an IV. You'll feel a little stick, but only for a second."

Beth tried to hold still. "How long will it take to get to the hospital?"

"Unless we hit traffic, be there in fifty minutes," said Gabe. "I tried to get helicopter transport, but they're grounded for the next hour. Thunderstorm's hit Dallas. Coming this way."

The pain came again. Low, sort of like a cramp, but different. Beth bit her lip.

"Another one?" asked Charlotte.

She nodded.

"Breathe slowly. In through your nose and out through your mouth," said Gabe.

She couldn't do it. Something wasn't right. Beth tried to sit up, but she was strapped to the stretcher. She struggled. Didn't he understand? She had to sit up.

"Easy now," said Gabe. "You're hyperventilating. Slow down your breathing. Relax. You're all right."

When the pain went away she stopped trying to get up. "What will they do to me? At the hospital. Will Dr. Lovington be there?"

212

"It might be Dr. Lovington. It could be one of her partners. Depends on who's on call. Soon as we get to the hospital, they'll put you on a monitor. If the doctor thinks you're having contractions, she'll give you medicine to stop them."

"What if they don't stop?"

"The medicine works really well," said Gabe. "There's lots of things they can do to help you."

"Beth, honey," said Charlotte, "when exactly did you start having the cramps?"

"I think after lunch. Treasure packed us tuna. I thought I just had an upset stomach. It didn't hurt that bad, and it didn't hurt all the time. When I got home from school, Sharita and Maggie and I hung out in my room. I think it was after you and Treasure left, when Ginger was there. The cramps came back worse than they were before. I went to the bathroom. Something felt weird. Down there."

"And that's when you called down for me."

Beth nodded.

"Does it still feel weird?" asked Gabe.

"Yes. Like something's there that isn't supposed to be."

"Medicaid?" asked the emergency room clerk.

Charlotte handed her Beth's card. Gabe, at the head of Beth's stretcher, waited for instructions as to where to take Beth.

"Need you to fill out these forms, please," said the clerk.

A nurse appeared. "You her mother?" Not waiting for an answer, she turned her attention to Beth. "You doing all right, sugar?" Then she spoke to Gabe and his assistant. "Gentlemen, we're going to exam room number eight."

"I'm her guardian," said Charlotte.

"Come on then. You can fill all that out in the room."

They were moving so quickly, Charlotte had to trot to keep up. "When did her contractions begin?"

"Sometime after noon."

"How far along?"

"Twenty-five weeks."

"Water break?"

"I don't think so. Is Dr. Lovington here?"

"She's in the house. We've paged her. She should be right down."

Charlotte held Beth's hand while her vital signs were checked, another IV was started, and she was hooked up to monitors. Under the bright lights, her skin was so pale it appeared almost blue.

"Hi, Beth." It was Dr. Lovington. She glanced at the chart the nurse had prepared; then her eyes went to the monitor. She snapped on gloves. "I see you're having some pain. Any bleeding?"

"No."

"Good. Let's see what we've got going on." She took a seat at the end of the table. The examination didn't take long. She stood up, dropped her gloves in the trash, and came around to where she could see Beth's face. "Your membranes are bulging."

"What does that mean?" asked Charlotte. "Is my baby all right?"

"I'm going to be very honest with you."

Please, God, Charlotte prayed.

"You're having premature labor. Your baby is in position to be born."

"But it's not time yet," said Beth.

"You're right. We're going to give you some medicine in your IV to try to stop your contractions."

"What if it doesn't work?"

"Then you will have your baby."

"Will she be okay?"

"Babies born this soon are always very sick. Occasionally they survive. Usually they don't. That's why we're going to do everything we can to stop your labor. We're going to start the medicine now; then I'm going to have you admitted to the obstetrical floor. The nurses will monitor you and let me know how you're doing. If all goes well, I'll see you in the morning."

Dr. Lovington left, and Beth and Charlotte cried.

Chapter Twenty-two

From the looks of things, Ruby Prairie residents had Tanglewood under control. Kerilynn and Ginger were upstairs trying to get the girls to bed. Nomie was cleaning up the kitchen. Dr. Ross was feeding the dogs and cats. Sassy and Chilly were prowling through the pantry to see what groceries needed to be picked up in the morning.

"Going after that boy?" Catfish saw Pastor Jock retrieve Kirby's address and phone number from the board over the phone.

"Yes. I'm not sure he'll be there," said Jock, "but I'm going to try to find him and take him to the hospital."

"Kid needs to be there," said Catfish. "But you don't need to be heading off on some wild goose chase by yourself. I'll go with you."

Jock attempted a stall. Was this a good idea? After all, it was Catfish's store Beth and Kirby had broken into for snacks on the night she ran away. It was also in Catfish's cabin that the two of them hid. And Catfish had been fit to be tied when he learned Beth was pregnant. He'd blamed it all on the boy.

"You sure? It's late. These kiddos right here need somebody to look after them."

"Shoot. They's plenty a folks to look after the girls. We need to go get that boy. He ought to be with Beth right now. Don't get me wrong. What that kid done was not right. But I've seen him around. Sticking by her. Heard he's been going to school and working two jobs. Appears to me he's trying to be a man about this."

Jock smiled to himself. He should know better than to be surprised by Ruby Prairie generosity.

"I'd be glad for your company, Catfish. The address I've got here is 413 Rock Creek Crossing over in Pear Springs. At least a good hour's drive."

"Maybe a little less. No matter. We best get going," said Catfish. "You reckon Charlotte's got a thermos bottle, Pastor? This is going to be a long night. We

216

might ought to fix us some coffee."

"Is the medicine working?" Charlotte whispered. She and Treasure had been dozing, but both of them woke up when a nurse came in to check on Beth—who was finally asleep.

"So far. It hasn't stopped the contractions completely, but it's slowed them way down."

"How's the baby's heartbeat?" asked Treasure.

"Doing all right. Slows a little when she has a contraction, but it picks back up."

"That's good, isn't it?" asked Charlotte.

The nurse nodded.

Charlotte and Treasure watched as the nurse pushed a button on the monitor and ran some kind of a strip. Then she took Beth's blood pressure and hung a fresh bag of IV fluids.

"How long will they keep her?" asked Charlotte. "I mean, if her labor stops?"

The nurse raised her eyes but didn't answer. When she finished her task, she motioned for Charlotte and Treasure to follow her out of the room.

In the hall she explained. "I think you've misunderstood. She's not going home. Her cervix is dilated and partially effaced. She's going to have this baby. We can delay it with medication, maybe for a few days. Best hope is for a week. We're also giving her medicine to speed the development of the baby's lungs, intestines, and brain, since we know it's going to come early."

The gravity of the situation slowly sank in.

"But she's barely six months along," said Charlotte. "Even if she goes another week—do babies born this soon survive?"

"They are very, very sick," said the nurse. "I'm so sorry. I want to give you good news, but I don't have any. Do you have any other questions?"

"What caused Beth to go into labor?" asked Treasure.

"We don't know. Mothers under seventeen are always at high risk."

"Dr. Lovington told us that. But everything seemed to be going well. Beth just saw her last week."

"Sometimes an infection causes premature labor," said the nurse. "Just in case, she's getting antibiotics along with the other medications."

"Thank you," said Charlotte. "I appreciate your being honest." She heard the television in Beth's room come on. "We better go back in."

"There's still time for a miracle," said Treasure. "I'm not ready to give up on this child yet. You go on in to her." She turned to the nurse. "Honey," she said, "which floor's the chapel on? I'm about to go one-on-one with the Lord."

Kirby, wedged between Jock and Catfish in Jock's truck, stared straight ahead into the night. Fifteen minutes ago he'd been sound asleep on his uncle's living room couch. Awakened by the two men pounding on the front door only inches from his head, he was still a bit dazed.

"You want some coffee, son?" asked Catfish.

"No, thank you." This was weird. He did not think he was exactly one of Catfish Martin's favorite people.

Catfish passed a cup to Jock.

"How long will it take us to get there?" asked Kirby. He was gradually becoming more awake.

"An hour and a half," said Jock. "Maybe a little longer."

"What exactly happened?"

"Nobody knows for sure. Beth was having some pains. Charlotte called for the ambulance, and they took her to the hospital."

"Is she going to be okay?"

"I imagine so," said Catfish. "Probably what they call that false labor."

"They've had time to get to the hospital by now, but I can't reach Charlotte. Most hospitals make you turn off your cell phones. She said she'd try to go outside and call us when she could."

"If it's not false labor, then what is it?" asked Kirby.

"It could be real labor," said Jock.

"Which would mean—"

"That she's having the baby," said Catfish.

Man. This wasn't right. She wasn't supposed to have the baby for another three months. He bet Beth was scared. He sure hoped it was fake labor and not the real thing. They'd only been to one of those classes. Six more to go.

"Charlotte told me Beth was asking for you," said Jock. "That's why we came and got you."

"Thanks," said Kirby.

"Are you scared?" asked Jock.

"I guess so." That had to be the understatement of the world.

Would Beth be hollering and stuff? What about the blood? "I don't really know what to expect."

"You're going to be okay," said Jock. "They'll tell you what to do. Mostly, you'll just want to hold Beth's hand and stay with her."

He could do that. For sure. Kirby sat up straighter in the seat. He hated that he wasn't at the hospital now. He should be. For Beth. And for the baby. This preacher guy was nice, but he sure did drive slow. "How much longer did you say?"

Charlotte brushed her teeth at the sink in Beth's room. She was grateful for the toothbrush, comb, and deodorant Kerilynn had thought to send her by way of Catfish. Too bad she hadn't sent a change of clothes. After two days, the pants and shirt she was wearing had begun to feel ripe. Had it only been two nights ago that she'd been out to dinner with Ben Jackson? Forty-plus hours since they'd arrived at the hospital? It seemed as though days and days had passed.

"You want me to bring you anything from downstairs?" Charlotte spoke to Kirby, who was sitting on the end of Beth's bed, watching her sleep.

"No. I'm okay. I'll get something later."

"You ready?" Jock, back from the men's room down the hall, stuck his head into Beth's room. He, too, was still wearing the same clothes. "Back in a bit," Charlotte told Kirby. "If you need anything—"

"You'll be downstairs," Kirby interrupted. "In the cafeteria. Got it."

"Treasure just called," Charlotte told Jock as they stepped into the elevator. "Said the girls are okay. Only problem is she's overrun with food. Folks keep bringing casseroles and Jell-O salads and banana bread."

Jock shook his head. "Not a bit surprised."

"You were right to send Treasure home with Catfish," said Charlotte. "All I could think about was how much I needed someone with me here, but she's exactly where she needs to be. Everybody's wonderful to help out, but they couldn't make the girls feel secure the way she can."

"I do think it's best she's at Tanglewood holding down the fort," agreed Jock.

"I feel bad about you staying on, though. I mean, I'm glad you're here, but I know you have tons of stuff you need to be doing. If someone from Ruby Prairie comes, you should catch a ride back. I'm fine. Really."

Jock didn't answer. He wouldn't have wished for this situation for even a moment, but being cocooned in the hospital, away from Ruby Prairie, together for almost two days nonstop, he and Charlotte had gotten to know each other much better. She could say whatever she wanted to. He wasn't going anywhere.

On the ground floor, the two of them got off the elevator and went into the cafeteria. It was open twenty-four/seven and had a decent selection, but the prices were high. Jock didn't feel all that hungry, but going for food was one of the only things that broke up the nerve-racking tedium of waiting.

"Jell-O again?" he teased.

"At lunch I had red. This is green. Totally different." She added a salad and iced tea to her tray.

"Of course." He reached for a ham sandwich. They moved toward the cash register. "How about we eat in the courtyard? Wouldn't it be nice to get a bit of air?"

"Any word?" asked Jasper. After spreading fertilizer on Tanglewood's acre yard, he had accepted Treasure's offer of coffee and a sandwich.

She sat down with him at the table. She looked tired.

"Where is everybody?"

"Girls are at Wednesday night youth group. They're feeding the kids tonight. It took some talking, but I finally convinced the ladies who've been helping out to go on home. They've cleaned this house top to bottom and done up every bit of dirty laundry. Somebody even washed the downstairs windows. It has been wonderful, but they have about worn me out. I need just a couple of hours of quiet."

"You want me to go?" asked Jasper. Maybe she'd asked him in just to be nice.

"No, no. I didn't mean you." She flashed him one of her smiles and rested her hand on his arm. "Please stay. I meant everybody else."

That was good to hear.

"You want some more coffee?" She got up and topped off his still half-full cup.

"Thanks." He wasn't used to being waited on. "When did you last talk to Charlotte?"

"I called her in Beth's room right before you came in. Not much change. Beth's doing all right."

"And the baby?"

"Holding its own."

"Charlotte is blessed to have you here," said Jasper. "Looking after things while she's gone."

"Blessing goes both ways. I love these girls. The Lord brought me and Charlotte together. Her grandma was a friend to me when I was a little girl. She looked after me and loved on me when nobody else did."

"Children need that love," said Jasper. "Especially these." He stirred sugar into his coffee, then lightened it with cream. "I guess you're planning to stay on here. At Tanglewood. You gonna sell your place in Oklahoma?"

"Been praying on it. I'm thinking I'll use the money to buy me a little place of my own."

"Really. But what about Charlotte and the girls?"

"I'll be here in Ruby Prairie. I've decided it's where I want to call home. But I'd like to have a house of my own. Have a room set up where I can do massage part-time. I can make my own hours and be available whenever Charlotte and the girls need me." She got up and brought him a piece of Italian cream cake. "I never did plan on living in this house long-term."

This was news. Interesting news. He'd not figured wild horses could drag Treasure away from this house.

"When you planning on doing all this?"

"It's already in the works. Been talking to the real estate people in Edmond about getting my house and business ready for sale. Got Chilly Reed keeping his eye out for a place for me here."

The woman was moving on this pretty fast. "He found anything yet?"

"Nothing like what I want."

"I wouldn't be in any hurry," said Jasper.

"I'm not."

"You never know what might turn up."

Outside in the courtyard, neither Charlotte nor Jock heard the page. They were putting their trays in the rack when they spotted Kirby's frantic face across the room. He rushed over, bumping into an older lady and nearly running over a little boy.

"Where were you? I looked all over. They called and called."

"We were outside," said Jock.

"What's the matter?" Charlotte already knew.

"They said her water broke," said Kirby. "She says she's got to push."

Chapter Twenty-three

"Listen to me." The nurse's face was too close. Beth tried to push her away. She needed room. There was pressure. Down there. Pressure unlike anything she had ever felt before. She held her breath and bore down.

"No. Breathe. You have to stop pushing. We're moving you to the delivery room. Don't push. Do you hear me? *Don't push.* Not yet. Come on. You can do it. Breathe with me. Pant like this."

"Beth, listen to the nurse." It was Charlotte. "Open your eyes. Look at me. You can't push yet. You have to wait until they get you moved. See? Here we go."

"I'm trying." Beth gasped and clutched at the side rail. She saw spinning colors and lights. "I can't wait. What's happening? Something's wrong. Am I having the baby?"

She felt the bed moving. It bumped against a wall. Someone cursed. Ceiling tiles blurred overhead. Faces, lots of faces, looked down at her, told her what to do.

"We're almost to the delivery room," said the nurse.

"Kirby. Where's Kirby? I need to push. Help me." She grabbed at Charlotte's hand. "I'm scared. I'm so scared. It hurts. Oh, it hurts so bad." She groaned. "I have to push."

"Your boyfriend's gone ahead," said the nurse. "They're helping him change into scrubs so he can come in with you. You're almost where you can push. Hold on just a little bit longer."

"I can't." Beth was sobbing. "Help me. Please help me."

Charlotte stumbled alongside the moving bed. She didn't let go of Beth's hand. They passed through a pair of double doors.

The nurse spoke. "Unless you change, you can't go

in. See that door? There are scrubs in there. Put them on. Somebody'll show you where to go. Better hurry."

But they were out of pants.

While a nurse went down the hall to get her a pair from somewhere else, Charlotte stood shivering in her underwear, crying in frustration and panic. It seemed to take the woman forever to bring scrub pants to the closet-sized room. She had no choice but to wait.

"Is she all right?" Charlotte heard Beth's voice when finally she was allowed into the delivery room.

"Tell me, is my baby all right? What did I have?"

"You had a girl," said the doctor at Beth's feet.

Across the room, Charlotte could only see the backsides of the half-dozen elbow-to-elbow doctors and nurses surrounding the baby. They spoke in low voices. Someone adjusted an overhead light. Someone else moved aside to make room for a member of the team who had just arrived. The bunch of them were so intent at their close work that their bent heads looked as if they were circled in prayer.

Beth was crying. Kirby, pale, with dark-shadowed eyes visible over his paper mask, was dry-eyed but dazed. It had happened so fast. In contrast to the noise and confusion of only minutes before, the quiet was disarming.

Wordless, Charlotte crossed the room and kissed Beth's salty cheek. "You were quick. I missed the birth."

"Only two pushes," said Kirby.

"I had a girl." Beth stopped crying. "Charlotte—did you hear? I had a girl. I can't believe it. Kirby. We had a girl."

"I need you to give me another little push," said the doctor.

"Can I see her?" Beth ignored his request.

"Need you to push," he said again.

Beth bore down.

"That's good. Very good."

"Is she all right? Can I see her?"

One of the nurses left the huddle and came over to give a report. "Beth, your baby's very small. One pound and seven ounces. You can't see her just yet. She's having trouble breathing. We're putting a tube down her throat and taking her to the NICU so we can take special care of her."

"But she's going to be all right," said Beth. "She's going to be all right, isn't she?"

Jock was waiting outside. Soon as he got the word, he began to make calls.

First Treasure.

"The baby's here. Yes. A little girl. One pound, seven ounces. Critical. Extremely critical, is what the doctors are saying. . . . Beth? She's all right. . . . No. Hasn't seen the baby yet. Probably won't for a few hours. She's in recovery right now."

Jock called Kerilynn next. She would pass the word.

"Everybody in town wants to help. What can we do?"

"Pray. Pray for all of us here," said Pastor Jock. ". . . No. Don't. I know folks want to see the baby, but for now I think it's better if people don't come. It would be too much."

Jock hung up. Knowing Ruby Prairie folks, now that the baby had been born and everyone was feeling the need to do something to help, Treasure had better get ready for a second onslaught of food.

The neonatologist, Dr. Cravers, came into Beth's room and introduced himself.

"How is the baby?" blurted Charlotte.

Dr. Cravers sat down on the edge of Beth's bed. She had been sleeping, and her face bore crease marks from the sheet, making her look every bit the fifteen-year-old that she was. Kirby stood next to the bed. He kept coughing and seemed not to know quite what to do with his hands.

Charlotte wanted to ask a million questions but willed herself to be quiet. Jock, standing behind her, seemed to understand. He put his hand on her arm, and she could hear his soft breathing near her ear.

Kirby and Beth were the parents. This was their baby. Not hers. She had to step back. They looked like kids, but they weren't. And would never be again.

"How are you feeling?" Dr. Cravers asked Beth.

"I'm a little bit tired, but I feel okay," said Beth.

"I'm your baby's doctor. One of them. There are several specialists who'll be seeing her too. You need to know, Beth, your daughter is very sick. She's unable to breathe on her own. She has problems with her digestive system. We're concerned she may have bleeding in the brain."

"Is she going to be all right?" asked Beth.

228

"We're doing everything we can for her," said Dr. Cravers. "Right now. But you need to know that very few babies born this early survive."

"But some of them do," said Kirby.

The doctor paused. "Not many of them do."

"When can we see her?" asked Beth.

"In about an hour, one of the nurses will take you in a wheelchair to the NICU. You'll be able to see her then."

This brought smiles from both Kirby and Beth. "I can't wait to see my little girl," said Beth. "We're going to name her Alexis, but we'll call her Lexi for short."

The doctor wasn't through. "You need to know what to expect. Your baby is very tiny. She doesn't look like a full-term baby. Her skin is wrinkled. Her head is bigger in proportion to her body than it would be if she weren't premature. She has a breathing tube in her mouth and a feeding tube in her nose. There are other tubes and wires attached to her."

Charlotte couldn't tell if either Kirby or Beth was comprehending what he said.

"I have a picture of your baby. I brought it so you'll be little more prepared for what you're going to see." He pulled a Polaroid out of a manila folder and placed it on the bed. The picture had been taken through a covered isolette. Mostly what could be seen was a tiny pink form covered with tape, tubes, and wires.

"She's so little," said Kirby.

"She looks red," said Beth.

The doctor caught Charlotte's eyes over their bent heads.

"Can we keep the picture?" asked Beth. "Or do you need it back?"

"You may keep it," said Dr. Cravers. "I'll see you and give you an update at least once a day. Sometimes things change with these babies very fast, so you may see me more often than that. If you have any questions and I'm not around, ask the neonatal nurses. They're very good at explaining things."

Kirby and Beth went in first, while Jock and Charlotte waited just outside.

It wasn't like the diaper commercials on TV. There weren't rows and rows of blanket-wrapped babies in open cribs. You could hardly tell there were babies there at all, because they were inside those covered beds. Which one was hers?

The lights weren't very bright, but it was loud. Lots of whishing sounds and some beeps. Did those beeps mean something bad? There were doctors and nurses everywhere. Busy. Some of them were doing stuff to babies. Others were talking to each other or looking at monitors and writing stuff down.

The nurse made her and Kirby wash their hands.

"You can leave the wheelchair right here," she said. "I'll help you with your IV pole. Did the doctor tell you what to expect?"

"He told us," said Kirby. He held Beth's hand.

"We know she's real little." Her baby. Hers and Kirby's. They were about to meet their little girl. Since she wanted to look pretty the first time her daughter saw her, she'd brushed her hair and put on lip gloss. Beth squeezed Kirby's hand.

"Okay then. She's right over here." The nurse led the way.

But her daughter was nothing like she expected, not even after seeing the photograph. Tiny and red didn't even begin to describe her. Was she even real? She didn't look like a baby at all, more like a just-hatched bird fallen out of its nest. Limp. Sort of wet. So many tubes. There didn't seem to be any place on her body that didn't have some kind of wire or tube attached.

Beth began to sob.

Kirby wiped at his eyes.

"Are you sure she's alive?" Beth choked out. "She's so still."

"Yes. She's alive, but she is very, very sick. She has a tube to help her breathe, one to give her nourishment, and IV lines to give her medicine and fluids. She has monitors to keep track of her heart and her breathing and her temperature. She's very sensitive to touch, but be very gentle and you can reach in and touch her hand."

Beth wasn't sure that she wanted to. Her nose was running. Her head pounded. Her knees felt weird.

"Can I touch her?" asked Kirby. "I'm her dad."

The nurse looked at him. "Of course. Let me show you."

"I don't want to hurt her or make her cry or anything."

"As long as you touch her very lightly, you won't hurt

her. And she can't cry because of the breathing tube that's in her throat." Kirby touched her hand with one finger.

"Can she hear?" asked Beth.

"Probably. So talk to her. Don't be afraid."

Beth wasn't ready to touch her baby, but she did have something to tell her. She put her face close to the isolette. "This is all my fault. It's my fault that you came out too soon. I'm sorry, baby. I'm so sorry. I tried to wait, but I couldn't."

The nurse put her arm around Beth's shoulders. "Sugar, it's not your fault."

"They told me not to push, but I couldn't stop."

"By the time you needed to push, there was nothing you could do. Your baby was going to be born no matter what you did. Besides, you did wait. You didn't have her until you were in the delivery room. You were very brave."

"I'm scared. I never had a baby before, and she's so little she doesn't even look real, and I don't feel very good. I think I might get sick."

"We don't want to overdo," said the nurse. "Let's get you to your room. You can come back later." She whisked Beth out, then called for a wheelchair and a nurse's aide to escort her back.

"Is she okay?" asked Charlotte.

"Just a little queasy," said the nurse. "She's been through a lot today. Pain medicine can make you nauseated. What she needs is to go back to her room and get some rest. The nurses there will give her something to settle her stomach."

232

"When can we see the baby again?" asked Kirby.

"Come as often as you want. Just check with the nurses on the unit. Let them know that Beth's leaving the floor in case they need to give her medication or check her. You can stay in the NICU and sit next to your baby's bed. If the doctor needs to do something or if she's having a test done, or we're having a crisis with one of the other babies, we'll ask you to step out. Other than that, you can be with her as much as you want."

Once they were back on the postpartum unit, Charlotte helped Beth get back into bed. Her arms and legs had never felt so heavy. She was thirsty, but too exhausted to even ask for something to drink.

"I wanted to stay, but I got so tired." It felt good when Charlotte pulled the covers up and tucked them in around her.

"That's okay," she heard Charlotte say as she drifted off. "Try to get some rest. You can go back and see her when you wake up."

Kirby was there when Beth woke. She'd only slept an hour, but she was ready to get up. How was the baby? She wanted to go see. "Where's Charlotte? Where's Pastor Jock?" She rubbed at her eyes and sat up in the bed.

"They're with the baby."

"Good. I don't want her to be alone," said Beth. "We should take turns staying with her. So she won't be scared."

Kirby nodded. He fiddled with the wrapper from a

233

drinking straw. "Do you—do you think she's going to be all right?"

"She has to be. She just has to be." She started to cry. "I know she just got here, but I already love her so much. I feel helpless. Like I'm supposed to help her, but there's nothing I can do. I'm her mother. But I can't do anything to help her."

"Can I tell you something?" asked Kirby.

Beth wiped her nose.

"I was a little mad when I heard you were going to have a baby. I was mad and scared."

"I was scared too."

"I didn't want a baby. I just wanted to have fun. But I never wanted anything bad to happen to it. I swear I didn't." He was crying now too.

"It's okay." Beth held him. "It's going to be okay."

"It's not okay. What's going to happen to her? What's going to happen to us? I don't know what I'm supposed to do. I don't know how I'm supposed to act. I feel so stupid, like I'm supposed to know what to do, but I don't."

"I don't know either. I've never been a mother before. We just have to do what they tell us. We have to pray that she'll be all right." Beth eased out of bed. "Come on. Let's go see her. I want to go see her right now. Can you help me? I need you to unplug this IV thing."

By the time Alexis was two days old, Charlotte had learned to dread Dr. Cravers's several-times-a-day visits.

234

They saw him every few hours. He never brought good news.

"Her oxygen levels are dropping. We are doing everything we can, but her lungs are failing."

"Your baby's heart is not pumping blood as it should. We have her on medication, but we're not seeing the improvement we hoped for."

"She's begun running a fever, and her white blood count is up. Tells us she has an infection. Antibiotics may help, but she may not be strong enough to fight it."

One by one, his words chipped away at hope.

Since Beth was now discharged from the hospital, she and Kirby were constantly in the NICU. Except for when they went to get something to eat or when they caught a few hours of sleep on the waiting room couch, they didn't leave. When they did tear themselves away from baby Alexis's isolette, it was only after being assured by Charlotte and Jock that they would stay.

"I don't know how to pray anymore," Charlotte told Jock. They stood looking down on the baby. "She is so sick. She's so little. And she's struggling so hard."

"I'm supposed to know just what to say," said Jock. "But I don't. She's in God's hands. That is all I know. That she is His."

It was just before midnight on the third day that Charlotte and Jock, on their watch, were suddenly told by one of the NICU nurses that they needed to step out. Charlotte saw Dr. Cravers reading a chart. Was it Alexis's? What had he seen? Did the man ever sleep?

235

An hour passed. Charlotte and Jock paced in the hall and watched the clock. It had been a long time. Had the nurses forgotten to tell them they could come back in? Would it be okay to knock?

It was then that Dr. Cravers came out. They should go and wake Kirby and Beth.

They needed to come.

Because the baby was worse.

Chapter Twenty-four

Charlotte watched Beth's face. Her eyes were wide. There were no tears. She clutched at Kirby's hand.

"Beth, Kirby," said Dr. Cravers, "this is hard for me to tell you, even harder for you to hear, but there is nothing more we can do for your baby. You need to know that it doesn't look as though she's going to live more than a few hours at most. Along with the other problems she has, which have been getting worse since her birth, she now has a large area of bleeding in her brain. I am so sorry." He shifted from one foot to the other. "It's time for you to say good-bye to your daughter. I've asked the nurses to take her out of the isolette so that you can hold her in her last moments of life."

Charlotte would remember the scene for the rest of her life.

The nurses moved them to an area of the nursery separated from the other babies. Charlotte and Jock were allowed to stay. Beth sat in a rocking chair. Though there were chairs for all of them, Kirby knelt on the floor beside her. The two of them took turns holding tiny Alexis. She wore a little cap and was wrapped in a pink blanket.

None of them could take their eyes off the baby. Charlotte wanted to hold her, but she didn't ask. Beth looked as if she never, ever wanted to let her baby go. It would not have been right to deprive her of even one second.

"I love you," Beth whispered. "I love you so much." Over and over she kissed Alexis's paper-thin cheek. "I am so sorry. So sorry you were born too soon. I'll never forget you. I promise." She touched the baby's hand, stroked her small foot.

"Isn't she pretty?" she asked Charlotte.

"She's beautiful," said Charlotte.

"She looks like you," said Jock.

"Mommy and Daddy love you so much," Beth whispered. "We love you more than you will ever know. We'll never forget you."

Four hours passed. Alexis's skin, already pale, began to look blue. Her hands and feet turned cool. No one said anything, but it was impossible to ignore the signs that she was getting worse.

Occasionally a nurse would come over, but mostly the staff left the five of them alone.

At four-thirty Dr. Cravers, with a nurse, appeared. He touched Alexis's cheek, placed a hand on Beth's shoulder. "It's time to let her go."

Kirby stood up.

"There's no turning back. We need to take the breathing tube out."

Beth nodded, but tears rolled down her cheeks.

"Do you understand?"

"Is it going to hurt her?" asked Kirby. "To take it out?"

"No, it won't hurt. Her body functions have already shut down. The ventilator is putting air into her lungs, but her heart is pumping so poorly that it isn't doing any good." He paused. "Once the tube is out . . . she'll be gone."

The four of them huddled close.

"Good-bye, Alexis," they whispered in turn.

The nurse began removing the tube.

"Please," whispered Beth. "Please. Oh please."

Slowly, gently, the nurse continued to remove the tube.

Beth, Kirby, Charlotte, and Jock all held their breath. Just as the tube came out, Alexis let out the only cry of her life.

Chapter Twenty-five

Pastor Jock conducted the graveside service three days later. He spoke briefly, read a psalm, and said a prayer. As soon as he gave his amen, Nikki and Vikki, Donna, Maggie, and Sharita released huge bouquets of pink helium-filled balloons. Everyone watched as the balloons shot straight up, then slowed to drift and twirl in the April breeze. No one in the crowd moved. A few sniffles were heard. When the last balloon moved out of sight, Treasure stepped forward to sing "Jesus Loves Me."

And then it was over.

Back at Lighted Way, where the ladies had prepared a mourners' lunch, the smell of homemade yeast rolls, baked ham, seasoned green beans, and scalloped potatoes teased appetites—even ones dulled by grief. Inside the fellowship hall, folks lined up to offer hugs and sympathetic words to Kirby and Beth.

"We're so sorry."

"You're in our prayers."

"If you need anything, sugar, you just let us know."

Charlotte and Jock, standing together, watched the two kids from across the room. Spending five days together in the hospital, sharing tears, meals, and prayers had broken down barriers of unfamiliarity between the two of them. They'd also spent the first three days of that week without a change of clothes, a fact that had certainly speeded up the getting-to-know-the-real-you-better process.

"How're they holding up?" he asked.

"I think okay," said Charlotte. "Something's changed between them, though. Beth told me last night she thinks that the two of them are just going to be friends now. She doesn't believe she has feelings for him anymore."

"After all they went through? I'm surprised."

"At first I was too. Then I realized that if not for the pregnancy they might not have ever seen each other again. The relationship was over. Or at least they thought it was."

"You think Kirby feels the same as Beth?" asked Jock.

"He says he does. I wonder. I feel sorry for him. Beth has a whole community of support. He has no one."

"He's a good kid," said Jock. "So many tough breaks. Doesn't seem fair. Any of his folks here?"

"No. He called his uncle. Told him about the baby, but he didn't come."

"Kirby'll go back to him, I guess?"

"Probably tomorrow."

"Does he need someone to drive him?"

"Jasper has already volunteered," said Charlotte. "Kirby's been staying with him since we got home. The man's been good to him. To my girls too. I think they've been out to his place riding horses nearly every day this past week."

"We need to keep in touch with Kirby," said Jock. "I'm going to drive over next week and see how he's doing."

"I know you spent time with him," said Charlotte. "I've wondered, is Kirby a Christian?"

"Yes, he is. He lived with his grandmother for a time when he was young, went to church every Sunday and was baptized. But then she got too sick to care for him, and he was passed on to other relatives. It doesn't sound as though he's lived with anyone of faith since he left his grandmother's house. There's lots he doesn't know or understand."

240

"I'd like to go with you," said Charlotte.

"Sure. I'll call you," said Jock. "What about Beth? What'll she do now?"

"Finish the school year. Relax some this summer, I hope. I'll be taking her for counseling. I suppose she'll start eleventh grade in the fall."

"So life goes back to normal," said Jock.

"Normal? I don't think there's any such thing," said Charlotte. "I'm just hoping to catch my breath before the next thing."

Charlotte made her upstairs rounds. Except for Treasure, who was still puttering around in the kitchen, Tanglewood was quiet. Charlotte peeked in on each of the girls. All were asleep except Beth.

Charlotte tiptoed into her room and sat down on the edge of the bed. "Long day, wasn't it?" She smoothed the hair back from Beth's face.

"I'm tired, but I can't go to sleep."

"You were very brave today."

Beth's eyes filled.

"You've been through a lot. Physically as well as emotionally. Your body's still recovering. It'll take some time before you feel like yourself again."

"I'll never feel like myself again." Beth lay curled on her side. "It's like that self isn't even here anymore." A tear slid down her cheek. "I miss Alexis. I should be holding her, but I'm not. She's gone, and there's nothing I can do about it. I know I messed up. With Kirby. But that wasn't her fault. God shouldn't have

241

made her suffer because of what I did."

Charlotte drew Beth into her arms. "Oh, honey, God didn't make Alexis suffer. He loved her. He loves you."

"I feel like He's mad at me."

Lord, give me the right words. Charlotte took a deep breath before diving in.

"God's forgiven you, Beth. Completely. He's not mad at you. The Bible says He separates us from our sin as far as the east is separated from the west. He doesn't even remember the things we've done wrong." Charlotte's voice choked. "How could He punish you or Alexis for something He's forgotten? The hard part is that even though He forgives, we still face the consequences of our mistakes. Your getting pregnant was one of those consequences. God didn't make it happen. It was the natural result of what you did."

"Why did Alexis have to die?"

"She died because she was born too soon. Because she was sick. Not because God was mad at you."

"Do you think she's in heaven?"

"Absolutely."

"I want to be with her."

"Someday you will."

"What if I don't make it? What if I'm not good enough?"

"You aren't good enough. Nobody is. That's why Jesus came. God loved us so much that He sent His Son. Do you realize God understands exactly how you feel? His child died too. For you and for me and for everybody else who wants to be good but keeps messing up."

"No matter how many times I hear it, I still don't understand. How could He do that? I wouldn't let my child die for somebody like me."

"Honestly? I don't understand God either. There's no way to explain a love like His."

Jock sat outside on his back deck sipping a soda, listening to the night sounds and gazing at the stars. Seventeen years of ministry. This had been one of his toughest weeks. He'd gone to bed early, but gotten back up when unable to sleep. Over and over he replayed the last hours of Alexis's life in his mind.

Kirby and Beth's mistakes had been costly.

Such suffering.

Such grief.

For two so young.

One thing was for sure. They must not let this event color the rest of their lives. Remember it? Yes. But not let it cripple them from living fully.

He'd talked with both of them this afternoon. At fifteen and sixteen they had their whole lives ahead of them. God had forgiven them, and they must forgive themselves. They couldn't beat themselves up forever or always be wondering what bad thing was going to happen next. Living forever with guilt and fear was not His plan.

Had he gotten through to them?

Maybe. Partially.

It would take time.

Jock chewed on some ice, fidgeted in his chair. He

crossed his legs, uncrossed them, then finally stood up and went inside. There was something he wanted, needed to see, an item stored in the closet inside his spare room. He ran his hand along the top shelf of the closet, groping until he found it—a slim, inexpensive cardboard photo album, one not touched since his move to Ruby Prairie five years ago.

He took the book into the kitchen, turned on an overhead light, sat down at the kitchen table, and turned to the first page. Twenty years ago. His wedding day. The bride and groom nineteen years old. She looking hopeful. He afraid. He'd looked at this picture occasionally over the years. This time he saw the pair on the page with different eyes. Compassion, not contempt, was what he felt as he studied their faces.

White dress. Borrowed tie. Homemade wedding cake. Thirty-dollar rings.

They were just two dumb kids who had made a mistake. He was a kid who would make many, many more.

Forgiven by God?

No doubt.

Forgiven by himself?

Not until now.

Jock turned every page, studying each photo in the book before finally closing the cover, returning to his spare room, and placing the album back up on the closet shelf. It was time to let his guilt go. Time—as he'd told Beth and Kirby—to forgive himself and stop living in fear.

Chapter Twenty-six

He bought rings. She bought a dress. Shoes. All new underwear too. The clandestine nature of their plans added to the already building excitement and romance. Even though it felt like torture to keep the delicious details to themselves, they'd decided it would be best to let everyone know after the fact. This was between the two of them. And God. Neither of them desired to hear even the most well-intentioned Ruby Prairie opinion.

Their secret would be public soon enough. Most folks, they figured, would be thrilled. Others, miffed at not being let in on their plans, would take longer to warm up.

Ten more days.

Then the whole town would know.

Everything had happened fast.

She still couldn't believe it was true.

They talked on the phone late at night. "You don't think we're rushing into this, do you?" she asked him again. It made her feel better to ask, better still to hear what she already knew he would say.

"We've wasted too much time already. You aren't having doubts, are you?" He pretended hurt.

She'd never doubted anything less.

There were lots of things to work out, details made more difficult because they couldn't be taken care of out in the open—at least not yet.

Finances. Bank accounts. Budgets. Wills.

His stuff. Her stuff. What they wanted to start out with new.

"We still haven't decided exactly what of each of our things we're going to keep," she said. "Maybe we should go over each room. Make some kind of list." Since one of their places was way larger than the other, she hadn't expected it to be so difficult. It was not until they began trying to decide what to keep and what to let go that they realized what a monumental task it would be.

Yet dealing with the material aspects of their lives was the easiest part. Of greatest concern was how their choice was going to affect the people they loved best. Some upheaval was inevitable. Likely a bit of jealousy. Perhaps a tantrum. Maybe some grief.

But not very much, they hoped.

Charlotte decided to celebrate the first day of June, in her mind the real beginning of summer, with a picnic on a blanket in Tanglewood's backyard. She set out a basket and began piling in supplies. Cups and plates— for seven, not eight, since Treasure was gone to Oklahoma to finalize the sale of her house and her business and wouldn't be home until late. Then napkins, chips, a new jar each of pickles and olives, and a tin of homemade cookies, brought over this morning by Ginger Collins.

She glanced up at the clock. The girls, invited to swim in Boots and Alice's new above-ground pool, wouldn't be home for another half hour. Great. She had time to run to the Quik Stop and buy fried chicken, which would be way better than sandwiches.

Too bad Treasure was going to miss the picnic. There was more than just the beginning of summer to celebrate tonight. She had a secret for the girls. A special surprise. Later tonight, folks from the church, to be let in on the news, were bringing over a cake.

Kirby had fallen asleep on the couch. When he woke up, it was to the sound of the five o'clock news on the TV and someone knocking on the front door of his uncle's house. He cracked the door open, saw a dark face, then realized who it was.

"Mr. Jones?"

"Hi, Kirby. You awake, son?"

Kirby pulled the door all the way open. "Sure. I mean, just a minute." He plucked a T-shirt out from under the couch and pulled it over his head. "Come on in. Sorry about the mess."

The place was a wreck. Stunk too. Mr. Jones sure was dressed up. Shoot. There wasn't time to pick anything up.

"Who's out there?" Kirby's uncle yelled from the back of the house.

"It's Mr. Jones. From Ruby Prairie," Kirby yelled back. For the past couple of months Mr. Jones had come and gotten him twice a week. Kirby didn't know why he did it, but it sure was nice. They talked and stuff, and Mr. Jones let him ride his horses.

Until today, he had never come inside. What day was

this anyway? Kirby wondered if maybe he'd gotten mixed up. Hadn't Mr. Jones told him last time it would be more than a week before he'd be back out to get him again?

"What's he want?"

"Nothing. He don't want nothing," Kirby yelled back.

"I came to talk to you," said Jasper.

Man. Kirby's palms began to sweat. What had he done wrong? He looked past Jasper, who was still standing in the open doorway. Somebody was waiting outside in the truck. Who was it? The law? Kirby couldn't tell.

"Son. It's okay." Jasper put his hand on Kirby's arm. "Nothing's wrong. I've come to ask you something."

Kirby sat down on the couch. Mr. Jones took a chair. "You live here with your uncle," said Mr. Jones.

Kirby nodded, aware of the Confederate flag tacked to the wall behind Mr. Jones's head, the empty beer cans that lay at his feet, and the sudden smell of burning weed coming from the back of the house.

"He's your only family?"

"Only one that'll let me stay with 'em," said Kirby.

"He's how old?"

"Twenty-six."

"How is it? Living here?"

"It's okay." Kirby stared at the floor.

"I see," said Mr. Jones. He fiddled with a ring on his hand. "I don't know how to say this, so I'll just come on out and speak my mind. I believe you're a fine young man. You've had some tough times. I reckon there're more tough times ahead of you, but right now I'm wondering if you'd like to come live with me."

Kirby's head popped up, and his mouth dropped open.

"I've got plenty of room. Ruby Prairie's got a good school. Folks are nice."

"You want me to come live with you? For real?"

"I do. After we talk about some things."

"Sure." This was unbelievable. Too amazing! Kirby was ready to pack his things that minute.

"Nobody's perfect, but if you come, I'll expect you to behave yourself. No drinking. No drugs. You'll have to work hard in school and help me out around the place. Brush the horses, put out feed, that sort of thing. Sometimes we'll have to work on the fences."

"Mr. Jones, I'll do anything you want me to do. I promise." He kicked at a beer can on the floor with his bare toe. "Those aren't mine. I don't drink."

He'd better not start out lying to the man. "I mean, I have. A few times. But not since—well . . . I'm trying not to now."

"I understand, son. What's done is done. I'd like to give you a fresh start."

"You don't know how bad I want out of this place."

"I think I do."

"When? I mean when can I—I mean do you want me to come now? Today?"

"That's something we need to talk about. I hate to get you excited and then put you off for a week, but that's what I'm doing. I've got sort of a good reason to need you to wait for a few days. Come on out to the truck with me for a minute, and I'll explain."

They hadn't been on the road ten minutes. "Stop," she said. "I can't stand it. Turn around. Let's go back."

"What are you talking about?" he asked.

"I can't get his face out of my mind. Let's go back and get him. Right now."

"But what about . . . ? I mean it's only our first—"

"Didn't it break your heart to leave that kid standing out in that awful, overgrown mess of a yard?"

"Yes. It did. But I thought you'd want—"

"What I want is to take that child home with us this very night."

Wanting the very same thing, he pulled off the road, stopped the truck, and gave her a long, wet kiss. Only then did he turn the truck around, put it in gear, and head back the way they had come.

Charlotte, back in the house for more ice, stood looking out her kitchen window.

Tanglewood's backyard was full of more than forty Ruby Prairie folks seated in lawn chairs—talking, singing, sipping on sodas, and eating chocolate cake. What had started out as an invitation for cake had turned into a full-blown party.

Donna and Beth, Kerilynn and Catfish were playing croquet. Nikki and Vikki were chasing each other with a pair of unfortunate brown toads they'd found under the gardenia bush. Ben, Boots, and Dr. Ross were pitching horseshoes. Gabe was blowing up balloons. Nomie was tying them off and passing them on to kids.

Earlier in the day, Maggie and Sharita had hung Christmas lights on the bushes and low-hanging backyard branches. From where Charlotte stood, in the waning light the strands looked like twinkling fireflies.

How nice it was to have a gathering at Tanglewood not associated with some kind of a crisis. *I could get used to this, Lord.*

Jock, stepping in through the kitchen door, interrupted Charlotte's silent prayer. "You ready to tell them?"

"Yes." She smiled at him. "I think now's a good time."

On the porch he helped her get everyone's attention. "Girls," he called, "come over here. Everybody else, too—could you move toward the porch?"

"Nikki," said Charlotte. "Put that poor thing down. Right now. Put it back under the bush."

"You should go wash your hands, sugar," said Lucky. "Toads carry germs."

"Yes ma'am." Nikki looked over at Charlotte.

"Do it."

Slowly, folks gathered around the porch at the bottom of the steps.

"Thank you all for coming," said Charlotte. "I hope you enjoyed the cake. And wasn't that ice cream good? Thank you so much, Ginger, for bringing it."

"My pleasure, dear," Ginger called up.

Charlotte took a deep breath. "I have some exciting

news." The group's ears perked up.

"So do I," came a voice from the shadows of the yard.

Who was that? Everyone turned around. Charlotte blinked in the light of the porch bulb. "Treasure? Is that you?"

Treasure stepped forward, parted the crowd, and bounded up the steps. She was wearing a dress. Ivory, with a V-neck and lace on the sleeves. Ivory stockings. Church shoes too. With little bows and delicate three-inch heels.

What was going on?

Out of the shadows behind her, sporting one of the biggest smiles she'd ever seen, popped Jasper Jones. He was wearing a navy blue suit and a sky blue tie.

Then Kirby came into sight.

"Go on," said Jasper to Kirby. "Go on up the steps to where she is." Not daring to miss a moment of something big, the crowd stood silent, at rapt attention.

"I've got an announcement to make too." Treasure gave Charlotte a hug so big it nearly knocked her over. "But you go first."

"I—I'm not sure what's going on," said Charlotte. "Why are you so dressed up? And Kirby? How did you get here?"

"Go on with your announcement," said Jasper. "We don't intend to steal your thunder; it's just that we've got news too."

"Well, okay." Charlotte still was confused. "Where's Beth?" She squinted her eyes.

"Right here," Beth called.

"Could you come up here?"

Beth moved forward to stand beside Charlotte, who put her arm around Beth's waist. "This has been a tough spring. In lots of ways. But tonight, we have something to celebrate." She gave Beth a squeeze. "Can you guess what it is?"

"No-o." Beth looked worried.

"I know how excited you were about going to school in Colorado. The good news tonight is that yesterday the admissions person from Wings of Gold called. They have a spot for you, and they want you to come next month."

Beth put her hands over her mouth. "Really? Oh my goodness. Thank you! Thank you!" She hugged Charlotte. Then Treasure. Then Charlotte again. "I can't believe it. I get to go!"

The crowd broke into applause.

When it began to die down, Treasure held up her hand. "This child getting back into that school is an answer to prayer. The Lord has been good to all of us here. Now I want to tell you how He has gone and been good to me. Folks—"

Jasper moved to stand by her.

"I'd like for you to meet my husband."

"And I'd like for you to meet my wife."

"What?" Charlotte was stunned. "You two got married? When?"

"This afternoon."

"No!"

The crowd went wild. Folks on the ground stormed

up the steps. Folks already on the porch swarmed around the newlyweds.

"Congratulations!"

"I didn't even realize you two were a couple."

"How did you keep this to yourselves?"

Charlotte noticed Kirby standing sort of off to the side.

It was Jasper who filled them in on the rest. "There's just one more thing. Kirby? Where are you? Come here, son." He put his arm across Kirby's shoulders. "This young man is Ruby Prairie's newest citizen. Treasure and I have talked it over with each other and with him. Kirby's going to be staying with us out at my place. He'll be going to school here in the fall. I hope you'll be making him feel as welcome as you've made me."

Charlotte and Jock sat next to each other in rocking chairs out on Tanglewood's now deserted front porch. Kirby and the girls were inside, watching a movie. Talking Treasure and Jasper into letting Kirby spend the next two nights at Jock's house had been an easy task.

"Thanks for staying, for helping clean up," Charlotte said.

"Glad to do it," said Jock. "This was quite a night. You okay with Treasure not living here anymore?"

"Sure," said Charlotte. "I never expected her to stay forever. Even after she decided to stay in Ruby Prairie, I knew she'd be getting her own place before long."

"I still can't believe those two had been planning this for—how long did they say?"

"More than a month. I'm so happy for them. I can't think of a more compatible pair."

They rocked in silence. Jock sneezed. Charlotte's chair squeaked.

Finally Jock spoke. "Jasper and Treasure didn't waste any time."

"No. They didn't," said Charlotte.

"Unlike us." Jock stopped rocking.

Charlotte did too.

"I'd like to change that," said Jock.

"Okay," said Charlotte.

"Starting tomorrow. Dinner? At Joe's? I hear his cousin the musician is back in town."

"I'd like that," said Charlotte.

Her chair squeaked again.

He sneezed.

Neither of them rocked.

"It's been a long time since I asked a girl out on a date," said Jock. "I'm not exactly sure what we're supposed to do next."

"I'm not sure either," said Charlotte. She looked at her watch. "It's getting late. How about we go inside? Check on the kids."

"Good idea." Jock stood up. "I'm wondering. You think there's any leftover—"

"Cake?" said Charlotte. She flashed him a smile. "I don't know. But that sounds good. Let's go see."

"After you," said Jock.

And together, they went inside.

Center Point Publishing
600 Brooks Road ● PO Box 1
Thorndike ME 04986-0001 USA

(207) 568-3717

US & Canada:
1 800 929-9108